D0834788

WHITE Lies

WHITE *Lies*

Sara de Waard

We acknowledge financial support for our publishing activities: the Government
of Canada, through the Canada Book Fund and The Canada Council for the Arts;
the Government of Ontario, through the Ontario Arts Council, Ontario Creates,
and the Ontario Book Publishing Tax Credit. We acknowledge additional
funding provided by the Government of Ontario and the Ontario Arts Council
to address the adverse effects of the novel coronavirus pandemic.

LIBRARY AND ARCHIVES CANADA CATALOGUING IN PUBLICATION

Title: White lies / Sara de Waard.
Names: De Waard, Sara, author.
Identifiers: Canadiana (print) 2021037151 | Canadiana (ebook) 2021037716x |
ISBN 9781770866492 (SOFTCOVER) | ISBN 9781770866508 (HTML)
Subjects: LCGFT: Novels.
Classification: LCC PS8607.E2363 W45 2022 | DDC JC813/.6—dc23

United States Library of Congress Control Number: 2021951285

Cover design: Angel Guerra / Archetype
Interior text design: Tannice Goddard / tannicegdesigns.ca

The interior of this book is printed on 100% post-consumer waste recycled paper.
Printed and bound in Canada.

Manufactured by Friesens in Altona, Manitoba, Canada in February, 2022.

DCB Young Readers
An imprint of Cormorant Books Inc.
260 SPADINA AVENUE, SUITE 502, TORONTO, ONTARIO, M5T 2E4
www.dcbyoungreaders.com
www.cormorantbooks.com

3 9547 00477 5925

To Isaac and Ava

… because I know that chasing my dream took its toll.
Thank you for your patience, support and love.

white lies
/ˈ,(h)wīt ˈlī/

plural noun

Harmless or minor lies, especially ones told so as not to hurt someone's feelings

Asking the Impossible

⋮

My legs are crossed, like a lady, apparently. The leg that crosses over my other leg sways forward and back like a Newton's Cradle. Constant. Rhythmic. Reliable; unlike my brain right now.

"Missy?" Dr. Tandalay looks at me from behind her crystal blue eyes. Clear conscience, I bet. She holds her gaze with the patience of a saint. For a moment, I engage in a staring contest. Who will blink first, I wonder?

Eventually, she blinks. I gloat, "Still the champ."

"Excuse me?" Dr. Tandalay is rightfully confused. It wasn't the answer she was looking for to this week's ice-breaker regarding how my therapy homework went.

"I used to play staring contests with my mom. Now that I'm older, I know she didn't stand a chance," I digress.

"Why?" she asks me.

"Because you blinked first."

"I mean, why didn't she stand a chance?"

I shrug. I don't dare tell a doctor — I don't care what kind of doctor she is — that my mom's bloodshot, dry, squinting eyes made her my helpless opponent. I definitely don't want to talk about how often she got high that last year she was still at home.

"Missy?"

"She blinked a lot." I end the subject.

Dr. Tandalay has this annoying tactic of waiting for my response way longer than an average person ever would. She gives me three times the "think-time" of the most well-trained teacher. So I always exercise my tactic of ... not answering.

Dr. Tandalay adjusts the lapel on her power suit and then jots something onto a paper that is clipped to a blue board with happy-face stickers all over its back. I find it all so distracting. The blue board doesn't make sense to me because it's a sad color, making the yellow happy faces seem contrived and ironic.

"Look, I'm sorry I didn't do my task." I mean it when I say it.

"Didn't? Or couldn't? There's a big difference, Missy." Dr. Tandalay does that thing with her face where her eyebrows read familiar disappointment, but her frown kind of gets me.

"I tried," I stretch the truth. "I know you assigned me to say positive things about myself, for you, but —"

"For *you*," the doctor clarifies.

"I couldn't, okay? Every time I tried to think of something good to say about myself, I felt like a fraud."

"Missy, you've been coming here for almost a year. You're close to sixteen. We still have quite a ways to go. One obstacle that is holding you back is the way you see yourself —"

I'm pretty sure that's not it.

"You are too hard on yourself —"

Who isn't?

Dr. Tandalay beats a dead horse, "There are plenty of wonderful things about you. It isn't lying, per se, it's being conscious of what you believe is the truth, until you can see the actual truth, clearly." She pauses, hoping that sinks in with me.

It drowns me.

"What are your parents like, Dr. Tandalay?"

She lifts her board to jot another note. The happy faces mock me. With each stroke of her perfectly sharpened pencil, they dance.

"Do you want to talk about your parents?" she asks.

"I want to talk about your parents."

"That would be a waste of our hour," she says.

I look up at the clock. "I only have five minutes left."

"Missy, I have an idea." She reaches into a side bin of small electronic devices and pulls out something the size of a Snickers bar. "This is a personal recording device. You just press this button to start recording your voice and this one to stop. I'd like you to re-try the same assignment, but so that you don't feel like you're talking into an abyss, you can talk into this."

"I can just use my phone." I hold up my cracked, ancient iPhone.

She pretends not to hear me. "Use this and try for one self-compliment per day. Do you think you can do that for me … err … for you, this week?"

I stare at her, without blinking, and play out our last four minutes with some think-time.

Trick or Treat

⋮

Mondays are my least favorite day of the week, but not for the reasons one might assume. It's because I see Dr. Tandalay every one of them and by the time the session is over, it's too late for me to head to the store.

So I have to head home.

I pop open the so-called childproof lid of my amber pill bottle. There's no need to read the label; I've been taking these suckers for about ten months now. I know the drill: "may cause drowsiness" (which is why I take them at night), "may cause dizziness" (which is why I don't like taking them), and "do not skip a dose" (which is why I set a reminder in my phone). You'd think I'd remember, but it's harder than it seems. Implicit memory — the kind you're just supposed to be good at, like knowing your left from your right — isn't my thing.

On Mondays I go to bed super early. Therapy exhausts me. Can I even still call it therapy since I have graduated from a therapist to a psychiatrist? I don't know if there's a new term. Psychoanalysis, maybe? I think I heard someone use that word before.

Almost a year ago, on my fifteenth birthday, I thought I'd entered *The Twilight Zone*. Trick woke me up at the crack of dawn with a gentle stroke of my light brown hair. He leaned in and whispered "Happy Birthday" to me. I was sure I was dreaming. His touches weren't usually soft. He was more of a tugger, a nudger, never a hugger, for example.

Trick is my father. His real name is Tim. Out loud, I call him the traditional "Dad" but in my head, I've reserved my right to call him "Trick" or "Treat." I developed this code as far back as I can remember — my first Halloween.

Like all youngsters, I didn't really understand what Halloween was aside from seeming like my universe flipped on its scary head for a day only to return to normal the next. It was the one time when suddenly no one was supposed to be afraid of monsters or aliens or zombies or blood, and if you were, people would just laugh and say, "It's Halloween."

Okay?

My father likes Halloween more than any other occasion. He revels in finding a costume and prancing around in it. His eyes light up when the pop-up costume vendors rent vacant spaces in the malls. I don't have a personal favorite costume of his, because I really don't like any of them, but I definitely have a least favorite.

I was four, and I was getting the hang of the whole unholy night. I looked at myself in the mirror, but could barely see out from behind my *My Little Pony* mask. I kept adjusting it for fear that

I wouldn't be able to see cars, like I'd been warned about on our school's morning announcements ... and don't even get me started on how petrified I was of potentially poisoned lollipops.

In the mirror-image, over my shoulder, a strange man snuck into my bedroom. His hat was brown and fancy, but he had burned, leathery, rippled skin. His teeth missing, *rotting*. His green-and-red-striped sweater. His sharp, far-reaching fingernail blades. To add insult to my mental injury, a scent floored me; a toxic mix of stale cigarettes and aged alcohol reached me before this monster did. I froze; hoping the creep would believe I was just an innocent pony and get the hell out of my room.

Instead, he snuck closer. One of his long, stinky nails tapped my shoulder. Bravery fled; I started to cry.

He laughed a maniacal laugh and tumbled off what little balance he had, onto me. We both fell to the floor. His cackling and stench suffocated me. I couldn't breathe; I didn't want to breathe. He was so heavy. I screamed for my mom as he laughed harder. Then when I screamed for my dad, he laughed so hard he couldn't talk.

The monster proceeded to tear off his face to reveal ... my father. "I'm Freddy Krueger!" he said so matter-of-factly, like I was supposed to know who — or what — that was.

Through terrified tears I uttered, "You tricked me!"

"That's what it's all about!" he laughed. Bits of his spit freckled my mask.

"I didn't know it was you," I cried.

"That's the point silly bird!"

Pony.

"You pretend you're someone you're really not for a while, just like you're doing!"

Nothing about me felt like a magical, rainbow-colored baby horse.

"You're so damn serious." He laughed and laughed at me until he puked a brownish-orange sludge all over my pristine, cloud-white costume.

From that day on, this would be a recurring thing in my life. Since I'd so frequently be unable to trust which side of my dad I was dealing with, Sober Tim became "Trick" to keep my heart on guard. Drunk Tim was a real "Treat," but at least I didn't have to wonder what was lurking around the corner.

And that stuck.

So then, back to my fifteenth birthday, when Trick woke me up with unprecedented ... I don't even know what to call it ... adoration? ... I was scared to open my eyes because if it were a dream, it was a pleasant one and I didn't want to bring it to a halt.

"Wake up, Melissa."

Melissa? No one had called me that in ages.

"Your mom and I want you to come to the kitchen. We have a big surprise for you."

About ninety-nine-point-nine-percent sure that it was a dream, on account of Trick saying that he and my mother would be in the same room, I opted to only half-open my eyes, hoping I could convince my brain that I was still asleep long enough to suck the marrow out of this fantasy.

I stumbled into the kitchen where my mother threw her arms around me and rocked me powerfully side to side, reciting a Marilyn Monroe-esque version of "Happy Birthday" in my ear. The husky, slow-tempo rendition was inappropriately sexy, but I let it go. Dreams can't be perfect.

I laughed, unexpectedly. Mom laughed. Trick laughed. What the hell was happening?

Mom led me to the table that was cleared off, for once. I glanced around for the rolling papers and pipes that I'd grown so accustomed to seeing in there for the last two years. I peeked under the table for empty bottles inconspicuously. Nope. Nothing around except for —

A homemade, lopsided birthday cake that was plunked down in front of me. It was one of the most beautiful things I'd ever seen. I just wanted to sit there all day and look at it. I wished I could take a picture of it. I wanted to Insta it; to show everyone that THIS year, my birthday was about ME again —

Not Jeremy.

My view of the cake was soon blocked by a massive, wrapped gift. I ignored the fact that it was clearly wedding paper, its silver bells glistened in the artificial light of our windowless kitchen.

"I wrapped it!" Trick boasted.

I nudged the gift to the side gently. "Did you make the cake too, Dad?" I knew he hadn't, but I wanted my mom to say she did. I needed to hear the words, to make this the sweetest dream ever.

"I made it," she said. Her words cascaded through me like pitch-perfect violin notes — interrupted by bangs on the front door.

My mom and my father exchanged glances.

"Open it!" Mom jumped.

"The door?" I asked.

"The present. Hurry up and open it!"

"Someone's at the door," I called out the elephant in the room.

Trick laughed nervously.

Mom folded her arms and shouted, "Open it, Missy!"

I reached for the gift. The bangs on the front door intensified; I retracted. "I'll go get it." I stood up.

My father pushed me back into my chair as Mom insisted, "This is your day, Missy. Open it!"

She was right. This was my day. Whoever was at the door could wait.

I pulled the gift onto my lap. In true form, I started to shake. Gift-opening adrenaline, no matter how infrequent, never ceased to consume me. I smiled again, despite myself. I took hold of a teeny piece of the paper and eased it back.

"Rip it!" Mom yelled, more playful than I'd expected.

I ripped it.

The front door tore open and two police officers barged into my kitchen. Just as I freed a MacBook from its silver-belled wrapping confines, one of the officers clawed it from my hands.

He tossed it to his partner. "Match its serial number."

"Give it back to her!" Mom screeched.

"Susanna —" Trick locked my mom into a tight hold to keep her from attacking the officer — which wouldn't have been her first time. This only made it easier for the officer to cuff Mom. She tried to wiggle free, but it was futile.

"It's time, Susanna." The officer said her name like he was family.

"What did she do?" I was no stranger to visits from the police for domestic altercations, but I had never seen my mom arrested.

"Officer, it's a special day, please —" Trick chimed in.

"I know, Tim." This officer was softer. "I know it's the anniversary of Jeremy's ... it's been two years since your son ..." He lost his grip on my new MacBook and it slipped smack into the middle of the cake, destroying the chocolatey bliss.

I mourned for my cake. I couldn't look at my mom; she wouldn't have met my eyes anyway.

This was definitely not a dream.

I should have known better.

Since then, almost a year ago now, Mom has been in jail. All because of a stolen laptop? My father and I never once talked about that morning. In fact, I've never talked about it with anyone. He has flopped from Trick to Treat over the past many months as I've tried to shut it all up with mandatory therapy and the meds that I just popped into my exhausted self.

The First Day

⋮

I stand as straight as I can in front of my full-length mirror. The top of my head is chopped off in my reflection. I've grown over the summer. No doubt I will still be the tallest in my grade, even taller than most of the boys.

Maybe that's what I can compliment myself on? My height. I pull out the little black, recorder thingy that Dr. Tandalay gave me. I press the right button, then open my mouth to say the words ...

I'm an idiot. I have absolutely nothing to pride myself on about my height. I don't eat properly. I don't stretch. Nature just kind of took its course.

I think a little longer.

I stare at my face. I note the freckle party on my nose and the way my mouth frowns naturally — my resting bitch face. I shrug and press the other button to end my agony.

I drag my feet down the stairs and pass Trick ... er ... Treat, on the couch, cradling an empty bottle of something on his chest. Out loud, because I know his life's blacked out at the moment, I voice this imaginary conversation with him:

"I'm off to school, Dad. First day of grade eleven."

"Isn't that swell, sweetheart."

"Yeah ... and I found this special, ripped and stained T-shirt at the bottom of my drawer. It's the only one that fits me."

"You rock that holey shirt, Missy!"

"Thanks, Dad. Did you make me breakfast?"

"You bet, sunshine! Peameal bacon, scrambled eggs, and sourdough toast, your favourites!"

"Mmmmmm. I can smell it from here. Thanks, Dad!"

Reality returns and I lean down to kiss my father's forehead. The stench of his hard-liquor exhale burns my nose hairs.

I walk into the empty kitchen, grab a can of Coke from the fridge, down it, and head out the back door.

I walk as slowly as possible as other students fly past me, eager to get to their first classes on time. Within minutes, the hallways are clear, except for me and a woman at the end of this one. I cock my head to watch her round the corner. I don't recognize her. The only people I don't know in this school are the ninth graders and she's definitely not a student.

I pick up my pace to follow her all the way to an abandoned row of lockers. She's darker-skinned with long, black hair that she whips up into a bun in no time. She doesn't know I'm standing behind her. I see her strip out of a really nice business-looking outfit, down to an extremely conservative bra and underwear, then into a caretaker's uniform. She turns and yelps.

"I'm so sorry," she says in a middle-Eastern accent.

I'm used to being the one who's sorry.

She continues, "I had trouble with my kids and their new nanny so that made me a little late for my other job and then it snowballed. This will not be a regular problem. Please keep this between us."

I look around for who in the world I would tell.

"I don't care," I say.

"Thank you," she says. "Who are you in for today?"

In for? Like whose face do I want to punch?

"I'm surprised to see a supply on the first day of school," she clarifies before I embarrass myself.

"Oh, no. I'm a student here," I say.

"Ah good," she relaxes. "Thank you for being a student."

"Thank you, for being a caretaker."

She stops dead in her tracks, as if I just told her she'd won a million dollars.

Her reaction hits me.

Maybe this woman can benefit from my therapy homework assignment much more than I can. I search frantically for something of hers that I can compliment. I spot her stilettos.

"Great shoes," I say.

She looks down at them, then up at me, and smiles. "Right? Thank you for reminding me," she laughs, seemingly oblivious to my compliment. "These just don't go with this fancy, navy blue uniform."

She hurls the shoes off and into the small locker with the rest of her outfit. She stuffs it all in tight, then shuts the door.

"Ahem."

We both turn to see Mr. Mianni, arms crossed, waiting for an explanation.

The caretaker starts, "I'm sorry sir —"

"She was just helping me find my first class," I interrupt. "Good attendance trumps crystal-clean hallways, right Mr. Mianni?"

"Don't start this Missy," he frowns. "We said you were going to have a good year this year."

You said.

"You're right Mr. M. I'm sorry, Miss …?" I lean into her to catch her name.

"That's Miss Maalouf." Ol' Mianni speaks for her, of course.

"Thanks for your help, Miss Maalouf," I say.

She smiles.

I head to a class that I could find with my eyes closed.

When I get there, I peek through the corner of the closed door's window to survey who else is in the class. Aside from your average bubblegum-blowing high schoolers, no one special.

"Are you waiting for an invitation?"

I turn to see who's talking to me. I don't recognize him. No. I'd remember this guy; his dark curly hair and pitch-black eyes confront me.

"No," I say. "Are you?"

We hear loud high-heeled footsteps round the corner. We look over to see a woman who I could recognize anywhere on account of the damn, bling-diamond cross earrings that eat up her earlobes. She's the Family and Child Services worker. I haul ass into the classroom before Ms. FACS spots me.

The classroom teacher looks over at us. Her shoulders drop.

"Missy," she says. She's disappointed. "And Luke. You two are late."

A wave of "woos" erupt from the onlookers, more interested in this moment than they will be in anything else for the rest of the day.

"I see my reputation precedes me," Luke says. "I didn't even have to introduce myself."

The teacher clears her throat. "Take a seat wherever you like," she tells us.

I resort to the seat nearest me and sink into it. Luke opts to sit on the back counter, by the sink.

"A desk," the teacher clarifies.

"I'm good here," Luke mutters.

The teacher pauses with the eyes of thirty-one students on her, all anxious to judge how she handles this one. She chooses to let this battle go. Instead, she re-opens her notebook and carries on.

I wish for a moment that I chose to sit on the sink first.

The Store

:

Tuesdays ... yes, Tuesday evenings are better than any parts of Mondays. I walk down the quiet street until I reach what has long ago become a safe haven to me: Ren's Relics.

I enter the front door of the stuffed, vintage toy store, like I've been doing since I was thirteen ... since the horrible accident actually. It was that night when I searched frantically for some kind of shelter to seek solace in. It took them hours to find me here that night. Not my parents, no, because that's the night they stopped caring about me. But the police ... the police barged in, assuming I was at that store against my will. Nope. Where there's a will; there's always a way.

Renshu, the store's owner, gives me his signature two-fingered salute when he sees me. He barely says anything to me. In fact, in the almost three years that I've known the man, he's managed to keep all of our conversations to inventory, prices, and general store stuff. I think he knows my name, but You seems to be his term of endearment for me.

Ren wasn't born here so when I first met him, I wasn't entirely sure about how well he spoke English until I'd heard him go on for hours about Marvel and Star Wars with a customer equally as fanatic about the stuff.

It's like there's no place for reality in this shop and that is, quite possibly, why I love it in here.

This Tuesday evening, like many Tuesday evenings, I'll do what I do, and what I've always done here. I lose myself in the mundane tasks of organizing, straightening, and cleaning the inventory on the shelves, extremely careful not to jeopardize their pristine condition. Once, when I dropped this Teddy Ruxpin talking bear toy thing, I thought Renshu was going to have a heart attack.

My OCD impulses calm at the sight of the straight lines I make; forward-facing action figures make eye contact with buyers. I breathe easier when things like the Atari games are alphabetized and color-coded. I exhale when, at the end of the night, I know that tomorrow's customers, or clients, as Renshu likes to refer to them, will be enticed and intrigued by the displays I created.

No one forces me to do this. No one cares if I do this. But this is the place where I escape, for a handful of evening hours, every weeknight but Monday, and most weekends.

Ren always leaves me stacked boxes of "new" goods at a small crook in the back of the store that doubles as its shipping and receiving area. I learned quite quickly of the world's strange fascination with these collectibles and I respect it, even though I don't understand it. Ren learned quite quickly that he needn't even open the shipping boxes anymore. My record-keeping of the items is impeccable and when I don't know what something is or what it should be priced at, I just research the hell out of it. Ren looks over my work for quality and control to make any necessary changes, but he never micro-manages me. He sticks to his talent for bartering with the clients who almost always make the mistake of thinking they know more than him. They never do and they leave the store being the first to admit it.

As I cut gingerly through the packing tape of the shipments, I love the clean, smooth slice of the X-Acto blade as it glides through like butter. And when all of the shipping boxes are empty? Damn. Smashing them to crushed, flat, lifeless piles of brown is one of my guilty pleasures. I perform a symphony of grunts and kicks in my euphoric isolation, until the last one is knocked out.

Ren gives me an approved breakdown of the retail prices for the inventory. I'm always shocked when his list gels so closely with my presumptions. Then, I proceed to put little, orange price stickers on the goods. Sometimes the value of the items requires very official-looking "Ren's Relics" cards that put shame to the teeny stickers. It all depends on the rarity and condition of the goods.

The most expensive thing we carry is this original Superman figure from the 1940s that is priced at $25,000! Ren has always been more of a Marvel guy, but his eyes light up when he passes this DC king in its glass display case. I've witnessed many clients try to buy it, even offering more than Ren's asking price, but when it comes down to it, he shakes his head and can't give it up. Not only is it the most valuable thing in the store, I believe it's possibly the most valuable thing in Ren's life, beyond his lost wife and his daughter Valkyrie.

Valkyrie scares me a bit. She doesn't look scary. She's beautiful, but she is an intimidating force to be reckoned with. There is no one in my small world of acquaintances who carries the same air of self-confidence as she does. Not even Dr. Tandalay.

I remember the first time I met Valkyrie, months into my daily visits to the store. She caught my pricing mistake on an item before I had the chance to look over my work — which I always do — and she lost her mind. She shouted something to her father in their mother tongue and he hollered things back.

They only resort to that when they're either talking about mundane things like, what's for dinner, or when they don't want me to understand what they're saying. I knew this was the latter because Valkyrie was pointing at a white bear Beanie Baby price that I forgot a zero on. Their words flung like a passionate tennis match. Ren motioned ultimately to Valkyrie's homework and then towards the stairs to their apartment. Before she obeyed, she approached me.

She was much older than me; a college student, but shorter than me. She noticed that I fixed my pricing mistake before she could point it out to me, but that didn't stop her.

"You need to be careful," she reminded me.

"I am careful," I whispered.

She didn't hear me. "That's Valentino," she pointed to the Beanie Baby.

"I understand," I confirmed.

"I don't think you do," she re-iterated. "Someone could have waltzed in here and bought him for nine hundred dollars less than he's worth, because of your carelessness."

"I always double —"

Valkyrie just put up her hand to stop me. "I've had him in my bedroom since I was born. He means a lot to me and I only want him gone when he's in the hands of someone who appreciates him and knows his value."

I just stared at her.

"Hello?" she asked as she waved her hands in front of my unblinking eyes. "Anyone home?"

Valkyrie was scolded with more Mandarin from her father as he pointed harder at the stairs.

She ignored him a bit longer and said, "My father says you always refuse the money he offers to pay you, for the work you do."

I nodded my head. "I'm not here for money."

"Then why are you here?" she asked.

For the same reasons she kept Valentino in her room, but my words stayed put in the pit of my stomach.

With an infuriated huff, Valkyrie turned and headed up to their small living quarters above the store.

She and I haven't talked since.

After the last of my shelves on this slow night, I walk over to my sitting stool behind the front counter. I never deal with the exchange of money or work the till — that's Ren's pride and joy — but I have this spot that he leaves clear for me to lay out my textbooks when I have homework.

As I sit here beside him, me concentrating on my schoolwork and him concentrating on a crossword puzzle, the silence irks me. Times like these, I tend to start rambling on about life, vent and spill the beans on people. I figure it's sane because I'm not talking to myself, but I'm comforted because Ren couldn't care less and isn't even listening. I speak:

"He isn't the cutest guy I've ever seen, by any stretch of the imagination, so that's not why I'm talking about him. I'm not even really talking about him, actually. I'm just talking about my day. And who sits on a countertop during class anyway? He just sat there the whole time and tapped the heel of his foot against the cupboard. Over and over. It wasn't really loud. It was just this rhythmic thump that I couldn't get out of my head."

Ren just plunks block letters into the little squares; he's a whiz with those things. I buy him more of them from The Dollar Store all the time. He two-finger salutes me every time I hand him a new one. It may not be the most responsible use of my weekly allowance; the whopping — wait for it — five bucks Trick gives me each Friday from his government funding. However, I like doing it.

Tonight's walk home is forgettable. Before I know it, I'm at my house and I don't even know how I got there. Dr. Tandalay tells me it's because I'm not present. She says that I escape reality and get so in my head about things that I miss out on the right now. I don't think she knows what she's talking about. All it is, is that I can't stop thinking about how tomorrow is the first Wednesday of the month and that the first Wednesday of each month is a visit.

In Through the Out Door

⋮

The soft, white ceiling tiles soften the profanities of the inmates, but can't silence them. The four-letter words puff from the ladies' mouths like rings of fire, blazing through the massive, concrete gathering space. But they fall on my deaf ears. I'm used to it. Nothing shocks me now. I may look like china in a bull's shop, but I'm a matador of life's crap.

There are about twenty tables in two groups in this visitation area. Rows on rows of social spaces for some of the most dysfunctional families in society. Tables and chairs rest nailed into the floor to lessen the chance of the furniture becoming weapons of domestic abuses. The guards couldn't stop an angry wife from unleashing the metal structures across her loved one's face if they tried, though. Knowing how little they get paid, their job dissatisfaction and the high turnaround, I doubt their tries would even break a sweat.

Except for George over there. George is the only guard I trust in this place and I love it when he's working. His salt and pepper, tight curly hair on his big, dark head comforts me. His massive hands mesmerize me as he does this rhythmic finger-twiddling thing, except when he stops to wave to me. I wave back and manage something in the realm of a smile.

"Something funny?" Mom asks when I reach the table for our visit.

"No ... no, I just —"

"How were your first couple of days?" she asks.

"Fine."

"Do you like your teachers?" she questions.

"It's too early to tell. Most of them just went over a syllabus and —"

"You never like your teachers anyway," she concludes.

I used to.

"What subjects do you have?" She leans in.

"Finite Math, Chemistry, English, and Phys. Ed."

She snorts, "Good. You need it."

A sharp pain strikes in my chest.

"Sit up, Missy."

I didn't realize I wasn't. I do.

For an uncomfortable minute, we don't know what to say to each other. In true form, what comes out of me lets us both down.

"So how have you been?"

Mom picks small pieces of lint off of her uniform green jumpsuit. "I'm in prison, Missy. How the hell do you think I've been?"

I look over at George's fingers. They touch, separate, then touch again like a familiar dance. He never folds them, always moving.

"Missy?"

"Sorry?"

"I asked how your father is."

"Oh. Yeah. He's fine, I guess. He's trying. He's looking for full-time work." I'm a fumbling football.

She snorts again.

"Times are tight," I divulge.

"Oh, and that's my fault?" she retorts.

"No, I'm just saying —"

"Save it, Missy. I don't need the stress of hearing about your tough times."

"Okay." I lower my head.

Mom's eyes well with tears; she puts her head in her hands. This, I cannot see. I avert my eyes back to George ... but damn it, he left his post, only to be replaced by some girl who's five foot nothing with the face of a baby lamb.

"Missy?"

"I'm sorry?" I'm an idiot.

"Look, if you're not going to listen to me, why do you even come?"

Because I love you. Except I just look at her.

"Fine. This is great. This was a fantastic visit, Missy." She bolts upright.

Lambie perks up. "Sit down, Susanna," she barks.

"Go to hell," Mom growls back at her, then turns to me. "Maybe every two weeks is too soon."

It's not.

"Maybe we can do this monthly?" she suggests.

Monthly?

"We have nothing to talk about, anyway —"

There's this boy.

"Guard!" she shouts.

Summoned, the guard moseys over and grabs hold of Mom's arm before she stands up. Protocol. The guard leads Mom back to the door that separates this visitation hall from the cells.

I ease the little recorder out from my pocket and playback the last bit of our conversation. My ears ache for words I never heard. My arms ache for a hug that never was. My heart aches for what may never be again.

All I can do now is stand my sorry ass up, show myself to the exit, and keep replaying our conversation like a boxer, beating myself up for the jabs I didn't mean to take and the punches I wish I'd just rolled with.

To add salt to my wound, on my way out, I see him ... Luke ... and his big, black eyes ... walking in, through the out door.

I slip behind a pillar to hide. Unbeknownst to him, we're the only two kids in this joint. Me, leaving a visit with my mother and ... him? Why is he here?

"Move it on out," Lambie McLamb urges me. I'm left to just wonder even more about the guy who sits on classroom countertops.

Great Shoes

⋮

Dr. Tandalay's office is busy on this particular Monday. I'm usually the only one in the waiting room. Well, "waiting" is a stretch; Dr. Tandalay is the most punctual person I know. She runs a tight ship and her staff is a well-oiled machine. The receptionist knows me without looking up. I tend to drag my feet.

"Hi Missy," he says, as he jots a note on his clipboard then puts it on the counter for me. His clipboard is different from Dr. Tandalay's with her chipper background happy-face emojis. His has some sparkly sequin accents along its edge. The small, silver circles catch the fluorescent lighting and bounce patterns across his face.

I know the drill. I grab a pen from the community holder and cringe. I hate these for-everyone utensils. I know this place is for "sick minded" people and there's no chance of contagion, as far as I know, but still. I sign my name, enter my time IN then hand-sanitize myself faster than the speed of light.

The receptionist laughs. "Never your favorite part, huh?"

"I don't have a favorite part." The words are more fatalistic than I meant.

"It's just a precaution," he says. "For safety reasons."

"Safety how?" I sincerely wonder, but I sound like a sassy almost-sixteen-year-old.

"Well, the name part is so we know which personality we're dealing with." His joke is inappropriately awesome, but I'm out of practice with my laugh, so I don't.

He clears his throat, "And the time IN, is so we know who's in the building in the event of an emergency."

"What kind of emergency?" a kid yells from the other side of the room. We both turn to look at him as his mother motions for us to please stop.

"Oh, well, not emergencies but like, fire alarms and stuff," the receptionist back-steps.

"Fire alarms?!" the kid screams, covers his ears, and starts rocking back and forth as his mom goes to work patting and soothing him into an eventual calm. I try not to stare, but I'm both shocked by the obvious trigger and jealous of the mother's patience. My dad would have hollered at me to knock it off. That's partly why he needs to be invited before he's allowed to come here with me anymore.

I turn back to the receptionist, "Nice one."

His cheeks flush.

"Next time, you can tell him it's in case a random shooter, armed with an assault rifle, waltzes in," I whisper.

He's about to laugh, I know it, but —

"Michael?" Dr. Tandalay calls out to the little boy, who looks up at her and recognizes his doctor. Dr. Tandalay waves him and his mother into her office. Then she looks at me.

"I'm sorry I'm running a bit behind, Missy," she tilts her head to stress her apology.

"It's fine," I say.

"No, it's not. Your time is important."

Geez Louise, I'm just trying to be understanding.

"I promise to be with you in just over thirty minutes. Are you all right with that?"

I shrug my shoulders. The little boy hugs himself around Dr. Tandalay's leg and, despite her professional attempt, she can't peel him off.

"Yes or no, Missy? Are you all right with waiting one half of an hour?"

I don't want to answer her. My shrug feels safe and enough. But I know she won't let it go.

"Yes," I say as my eyes yearn to roll back in my head.

Dr. Tandalay nods and turns to her session door. She gives way to Michael's mother then with as much dignity as she can muster, she drags Michael along inside too.

I turn to the receptionist. "I guess it's just me and you."

He nods.

"And the other me," I joke.

He gets it, and laughs. Hard.

I take a seat in the now empty waiting room and ... wait.

❖

"So let me paraphrase what I think you're saying," Dr. Tandalay leans closer to me. "You believe that your mother doesn't want you to visit her as frequently?"

"This isn't just something I arbitrarily believe, Dr. T. She said it. Monthly, she said," I clarify. I would replay it for her, but I don't think she'd approve of my use of the device she lent me.

Dr. Tandalay frowns.

"It's okay, though. I mean, the visit didn't go particularly well, but ..." I digress.

"You have every right to be upset, Missy," she stresses.

"I'm not upset," I say.

"Missy —"

"Hey guess what? I did my homework." Me ... the Master of Re-Direction.

Dr. Tandalay doesn't want to bite, I can tell, but she's also slightly shocked by my update, so she's conflicted. Bite the bait or excavate?

"You did?"

Yes, winner.

I stretch the truth. Well, actually, I stretch, pull, yank, grab, tear, mangle the truth.

"Yep," I gulp.

"You complimented yourself?" She's in disbelief.

I think of the caretaker, Miss Maalouf, and her great shoes. A smile escapes me. Dr. Tandalay makes a note and I swear the happy faces on the back of her clipboard *tssk tssk* me.

"That's an excellent step, Missy." She smiles. "You haven't fed yourself much positivity since I've known you. Tell me about it."

The thing is, it really wasn't hard to compliment someone else.

The cold, hard truth is, I don't need to compliment myself. Dr. Tandalay has this one wrong. I'm sure of it. So, I make crap up.

"Well, I looked at myself in the mirror, and at first, I did that thing you taught me to do … the thing where I look around the room and find five things in five colors to calm myself down —"

"You grounded yourself," she reiterates.

"Yeah, I grounded myself, which I think is a weird way of saying it because up until I met you, being grounded was a bad thing."

"Would you prefer I call it mindfulness?"

I shrug.

She goes to scold my shrug —

"No," I say. "It doesn't matter what we call it. I don't care."

"Okay, so first you grounded yourself," Dr. Tandalay says to move us along.

"Yes. Then, I looked myself dead in the eyes and then it hit me …" Maybe that was a bit too dramatic, so I tone it down. "I just told myself that I'm smart."

"Smart … and?" she waits.

"And another time I told myself I'm nice, to some people." An image of Ren's crosswords flashes before my eyes.

"Smart. Nice. And?"

Jesus, woman. What do you want?

"And one day I even told myself I looked pretty." I throw up in my mouth a little.

Dr. Tandalay takes a few more notes. "How did these exercises make you feel?"

"Great!" My voice cracks.

Dr. Tandalay stares at me. The awkward silence makes my armpits sweat.

Then she smiles a soft smile and adds one more note to her paper. "Okay, Missy. Our time is up for this week."

"Oh, that's too bad." Hot damn; I'm on a roll. I stand up.

"I do have a new homework assignment for you, though," she adds.

I sit back down. "Sure thing."

"Since you're making gains with positive self-talk, this coming week I'd like you to not only keep saying nice things about yourself, but actually do some nice things for yourself."

"Easy," I toss the word.

"Oh really? When was the last time you did something nice for yourself?"

Crickets.

Sanitation Crew

⋮

Sitting in this English class always makes me feel a little drowsy, but today more than ever. I glance around the room while my teacher lectures us on *Romeo and Juliet* with particular attention paid to the metaphor of Juliet being the sun. She prompts the class for a response to her question.

"So why did Shakespeare use the sun?"

I find it somewhat amusing to watch twenty-eight students lower their eyes as soon as the teacher's question leaves her lips. No one wants to be called upon. Everyone wants to just sit and keep to themselves. A wrong answer will get you laughed at later. A right answer will pigeonhole you as a suck up. And heaven forbid you're called on without even raising your hand because hell, then you're outed as the teacher's pet.

So I just stare at my teacher. It works. She never calls on me.

"Missy?"

Oh gawd.

A couple of people snicker. Luke, who is seated in the middle of nowhere, confined to a desk, but definitely in a made-up row, turns to look at me.

I feel my cheeks redden and my stomach does a wonky flip flop.

Why the sun? What a stupid question. Juliet is the sun because without her, Romeo is dead. It's symbolic and also foreshadowing. We all know good ol' Romeo does himself in when he thinks he's lost his precious flower.

"Missy?" the teacher asks again.

But I don't want to answer and I want to tell Luke to stop staring at me with those stupid black eyes of his. He finally takes his eyes off me to look at his phone. Then he looks up at the clock, stands up, and walks out of the room. The teacher doesn't stop him; she just keeps me cornered.

"Why ... the ... sun, Missy?"

The classroom door slams shut behind Luke. A couple of people jump.

"Look, if you don't know the answer, just say so," the teacher huffs.

I want to tell her to go stuff herself. I open my mouth to follow through on my instinct, but a sharp pain twinges my lower insides.

I raise my hand.

She rolls her eyes. "Yes, Missy? The sun?"

"I have to use the restroom," I say.

A girl beside me laughs. I shoot her the stink eye.

"I'm not falling for that one." The teacher crosses her arms.

"There's nothing to fall for. I sincerely need the restroom,"

I say. I can feel my body failing me now. Right here. In the middle of English class. I know my period has come. I also know I wasn't prepared for it.

"You can see your ... friends ... anytime Missy." The teacher assumes I want to chase old black eyes out the door. "Answer the question."

Oh, what to do? What to do?

I stand up.

"Sit down," the teacher orders.

A girl from the back of the room reacts to what I can only assume is a big bloody blotch on the crack of my jeans. She grabs her sweater and hands it to me.

"It's cool," I say. "I don't want to ruin it."

My teacher isn't the sharpest knife in the drawer, but eventually reads the situation right. She freezes in awkwardness.

I pick up my binder and pens and bend down as gracefully as I can, to minimize the trauma to the boys in the class who won't be able to un-see this for quite a while. I grab my backpack, hold my head as high as I can, and walk between the tight rows of desks. It's times like these that I wish I weren't so damn tall as my backside aligns perfectly with the curious stares of onlookers.

I salute the teacher as I exit with dwindling dignity.

Ah, the joys of the high school Lost & Found, a cemetery of forgotten trinkets and whatnots. Broken pencils poke through abandoned toques and single socks, ripped T-shirts and rotten gym shorts. I dig with disdain, rummaging through with the expertise and impatience of an old lady at a DVD sale bin in Walmart.

I hold up a pair of faded blue jeans that have probably been in this bin long enough to be back in style. Nope, upon closer look, they're wretched. The scrunched, elastic-band waist is twisted in many places. The zipper's teeth are missing like a 1950s goaltender's. The pockets are fake and the faded knees sport grass stains.

"Slim pickings," I mutter to myself. I eye how far away the girls' washroom is and note how many open classroom doors I'd need to walk by. Instead, I drop my pants then and there, do a quick-change, and hope no one was hurt in the making of this. I'm no Clark Kent. I stick a hopefully-absorbent toque down my new pants and into my undies. That'll do ... for a little while at least.

I'm in familiar territory: the office. I'm rarely here by any fault of my own, but I'm here a lot.

They say the office is the heart of the school, but I disagree because I believe it's more like the butthole of the school. And I'm proven right when I sit down only to see Luke stationed further down the bench from me. I don't know if he sees me; he doesn't look up. His eyes fixate on his phone on his lap.

"Phone away, Luke," Mr. Mianni barks from his Principal's Office, using the vision at the back of his head, apparently. Luke laughs and continues to tap away at some game I can't quite get a good look at.

Out of the corner of my eye, I see Miss Maalouf struggle to carry a mop and my bloodied chair down the hallway. Red from the chair smudges her weight-bearing, uniformed hip. I cringe; that's not going to be easy to get out.

My attention is called upon by a familiar, high-pitched, inauthentically chipper voice.

"Hello, Melissa," Ms. FACS calls out.

"I prefer Missy, Ms. FACS," I correct her. Luke looks up.

"I know you know my name is Priscilla." She smiles, like we're old pals.

"I know you know I prefer to be called Missy." I smile too, through clenched teeth. Luke laughs a bit. Priscilla and I both ignore him.

Priscilla whispers, but her voice is still squeaky. "Why didn't you have ... something?"

I choose not to whisper. "I just forgot."

"Do you have adequate supplies at home?" she whispers.

"Pads and tampons?" I blurt out. Luke looks over.

"Missy?" Priscilla bends down to be eye-level with me, like I'm a five-year-old or something. Those huge, diamond cross earrings of hers catch a ray of light. "Do you have the supplies you need?"

No. But I nod yes.

"Do you need help marking a calendar with an idea of when it will happen again?" I can barely hear her, she's so quiet.

Yes. But I nod no.

Truth is, I have no idea when it's going to come. I know the math. I know the science. I know it should come around twenty-eight days from the time it last started. I know that in the middle, around day fourteen, I'm my most fertile. Not like there's any chance I'm pregnant — never had sex. Probably never will. But since all the stress of Jeremy's death and the part I played in it, my body doesn't know how to get into any kind of routine. Anytime can be Surprise Time and there's no way I'm wearing a pad or tampon every flipping day waiting for it like some kid in line at Canada's Wonderland.

That, and my father never buys the stuff I need. He barely buys me food, let alone absorbent, wafer-thin things with wings to soak up the blood of his teenaged daughter, especially when all he can think about is how much he misses his damn son.

"So your dad is on top of those things these days?" Priscilla pries.

"Can I just go get something from the back room now? To hold me over? I feel like I have a beaver dam lodged in my crotch."

Luke bursts out laughing.

Priscilla blushes. She stands as tall as she can and motions for me to go ahead.

I stroll past her, then Luke, and head right into the back room of stacks of photocopy paper, dusty art supplies, spare desks, spilled Band-Aids, and, alas ... pads. Pads that are way too thick and more budget than No Name, but pads nonetheless. I grab enough to last me the week and hide them on me, wherever I can find spots.

As I walk out of the room, I notice that Luke is gone. I watch Miss Maalouf scrub the side of her uniform. She looks up at me and then looks down, at my jeans. She frowns. She motions for me to follow her out and all the way to her locker. She opens it. I memorize her padlock code. Not because I would ever break into it, but because I can. I'm just good at stuff like that for some reason ... plus, most people are pretty bad at hiding their information.

Miss Maalouf points to her nice clothes, a money pair of pants, in particular. "Those should fit," she says.

"Oh, no, I'm good," I say.

She tugs at the fake pocket of my lost and found jeans, and laughs.

"Okay fine," I agree. "But only because I know you want to borrow these suckers from me."

Do Something Nice for Yourself

⋮

It's a quiet night at the store. Ren sits in the corner, behind the counter, and watches his Mandarin soap-opera. He chuckles every now and again at something that must be funny. When a commercial comes on, sometimes he looks over at me to two-finger salute and smile. I can't help but smile back.

He often seems like he's at a loss for words in the rare instances that he talks to me. It's like he stutters with me, but is as eloquent as a Ted-talker with everyone else, English or Mandarin.

He hesitates a few times then says, "The ETs look lonely."

I peek over at the ten, three-foot tall extra-terrestrial, alien dolls. They look fine to me. "We don't have any Elliott's," I say.

"I suggest you mingle some other things in there," he says.

"Nothing else really makes sense," I answer.

"It's acceptable if the figures don't go together, traditionally. I just don't prefer for them to look so isolated up there," he reiterates.

I look at Renshu then back at the ETs — staring back at me with their massive blue eyes that until this very moment, never appeared sad to me. "Okay boss," I relent.

I walk over and spend the next while adding some other figurines and toys to the section. My OCD compels me to at least make sure the other choices are in the space realm or else I won't sleep tonight.

"All good," I give my thumbs-up when I'm done. It's our usual ten-four.

He goes back to his regularly scheduled programming and the silence billows. I bring up Luke again, for some reason.

"You know that new guy?" I start. Ren barely takes his eyes off the screen, but I see a flicker of a side look. I feel fine to continue. "Well, he never talks to anyone and he does his own thing all the time, like he owns the place."

Ren tidies things on his side of the counter, making all kinds of racket while I carry-on my one-sided conversation. "I saw him talking to Ms. FACS this afternoon so of course I'm wondering why. And, get this, I saw him at the penitentiary the other day!" I look over at Ren, expecting shock, but I don't get any. "I want to know who he was there to see. Like, is his mom there too? I mean, that would be super weird, but who else would he be in there to see? Maybe a grandma or a sister? Can you imagine how weird that would be to have a grandma in jail, Renshu?"

He looks up at the sound of his name only to reach for his record-keeping books to track today's sales.

"Well, I'm going to ask him, soon. I'm not scared to. Why would I be scared? He's just a guy. He's nothing special. There's no reason why I wouldn't. No reason I can't. I just ... haven't had the time yet. I'm busy with school and stuff and I have to concentrate now that I'm in grade eleven."

Ren's show comes back on. He's not conflicted. He doesn't feel the obligation to stay tuned to this teenaged girl's spitballing. He returns to his fantasy world of the dysfunctional melodrama of perfectly pretty people.

Not long after, a customer rushes in. A mini-customer shuffles in a few steps behind her. I assume it's a mother and son duo by the way the woman holds her hand out slightly behind her ... you know ... that way many moms do it? They walk ahead of you slightly, but their arm is extended back, perpetually offering a hand to their offspring. My mom used to do that to Jeremy. I remember that. But I don't remember the last time she did it to me.

The boy ignores the gesture though. Not out of spite, he's just too in awe of the wonder world of toys. He beelines it for the Hot Wheels display and picks up one of the cars that isn't protected in original packaging. He vroom-vrooms it along the edges of the shelves, down his arm and over an imaginary death drop of doom. He puffs up his cheeks and lets out bits of air each time the car rounds a corner.

I get a lump in my throat. From the back, the kid looks just like my brother did. I try to distract myself with the foreign absurdities of Ren's television show.

The mother rushes up to the counter. "I'm in a hurry," she gasps. "We have a birthday party for an eight-year-old who likes toys.

I don't have time to go all the way to Walmart." She wants to stick her foot in her mouth when Ren's disappointment floods his face. "I'm sorry, I mean ... I think your stuff is great but I just ... I just don't usually have a budget for —"

"I have just the thing," Ren stands up and leads the woman to an aisle.

Mere moments later, the mom plunks her purchase onto the counter. I look at her choice: a Batman figure with a Robin companion. I'm surprised frankly. This mom alludes to financial struggle and then picks a $200 gift?

The woman presses me with her eyes to ring the thing in, but I wait until Ren is back behind the counter and he does it. Out of the corner of my eye, I see Ren scrunch up the item's fancy price card in his hand, and toss it under the counter.

"Thirty-five dollars, please," Ren coughs up.

The mom opens her wallet and picks through a very small pile of bills. "I was really hoping to keep it under twenty-five," she pleads with as much dignity as she can muster.

I look at Renshu. I'm curious what he's going to say, but not really surprised when he says it. "That will suffice."

"Thank you," she says. "You definitely can't do that at Walmart," she calls it back as a joke. Only I laugh. She has no idea of what happened here, other than thinking she just saved herself ten bucks. "Joey, we're all set," she calls out to her son.

Joey obeys without hesitation. He walks over and stands next to his mom, except his hands aren't empty. I see that he has two little Hot Wheels in his hands. They aren't protected vintage, but vintage, nonetheless.

"Mommy?" he says.

She doesn't hear him. I mean, she probably "hears" him, but it doesn't register. She's busy gathering her wallet, the toy, and her receipt.

"Mommy?" Joey tries again, patient but consistent.

"What's up, Bub?" she asks while tucking the receipt into a compartment of others in her wallet.

"Can I please buy these?" Joey holds up the two toy vehicles. One is a red truck. A flash of my mom's old, huge, red truck runs through my mind. I drop the pen I was holding.

"No dude, sorry. You can add them to your list, though." The mom cringes.

"I don't need you to buy them, Mommy. I will do it." Joey is pragmatic. "With my money under my mattress."

The mom is really all set now and she turns to go, extending back her faithful hand.

"Mommy?" Joey reminds her, as if she isn't fully aware.

"No, Joey. You only have a few dimes under your mattress. That's not enough money."

"What about the ones I have in Woody?" he asks.

"Those are old-fashioned pennies. One cents."

"I have so many of those," he boasts to me.

I smile. The lump in my throat expands. He's missing his two front teeth just like Jeremy was.

"Pennies are pretty much worthless." I'm sure she didn't mean to crush him, but she did. Joey's shoulders slump as he takes the two toys back to their shelf.

My stomach hurts. Not in an over-ate or period kind of way. In a way like I'm being pulled and twisted into knots. If I were this kid, I'd be so pissed. But here he is, taking life's crap like a little champ.

The two of them walk out of the store's door as its bells jingle all the way into my soul.

I look at Ren, who appears oblivious. Then I look over at the Hot Wheels shelf.

I jump over the counter like the gazelle my height intended for me to be and grab the toys of Joey's liking. I burst out the door and look both ways for the kid and his mom. I spot them, just up the street.

"Hey Joey," I call out. He looks over at me and shields his eyes from the sunlight. His mother looks up at me like I look at department store workers when their alarms go off as I exit, even though I know full well that I haven't stolen anything.

"I have an idea," I say as I invade his personal space. It's uncomfortable for me and I can only imagine how it feels for him, but I hope my creepiness pales in comparison to my proposition.

"Are these the two that you wanted?" I ask him as I hold my hands out. Joey looks at the Hot Wheels. I feel his hesitation. I know this hesitation. It's the hesitation of someone who is so used to dealing with disappointment that learned helplessness takes over — a defense that prepares kids for the bitter so that anything remotely above it seems sweet.

Alas, Joey nods.

"Well, today is your day, little man." The term of endearment rolls off my tongue with the same ease it used to for Jeremy. So I bite it. Hard. I won't make that mistake again. I continue, "We have a layaway plan at the store."

Most people my age wouldn't know what a layaway plan is, but then again, most don't have to deal with the likes of my father, who, at any opportunity he gets, asks store managers about their Layaway Plan. Embarrassment washes over me every time they go over the lengthy terms and interest details, trading his soul for putting his purchase in holding while he makes little payments on it until he can bring it home.

"Joey," I say, "if you promise to pay me a little bit of money at a time, these can be yours, today."

"Really?" Joey's eyes are lighthouse beams; looking over the toys, then back up at me, then back at the toys.

"He can't do that." His mom's words are the perfect storm.

"Oh, our terms are very gentle, ma'am. Joey can literally pay what he can, when he can. No terms. No interest," I wink at her. It's such a grown-up gesture and I feel like I've been possessed by Oprah Winfrey or something as I try to negotiate how best to make this kid's day. "Joey, do you think you can do that?" I ask him.

"Pay what I can ... when I can?" he ponders. "Yes!" He reaches his little hands out for the toys.

"This isn't realistic. It's teaching him a terrible lesson," the mother huffs as she holds out her hand for Joey's. "Let's go."

"Well, I'm inclined to just give them to him and pay for them myself," I say. "But I know for sure that that definitely isn't teaching him anything." I talk to her more privately, "I know what you mean and I respect where you're coming from, but please, can we meet somewhere in the middle? I'd like to do something ... nice, for him." Dr. Tandalay's face flashes before my eyes.

"Please, Mommy?" Joey pleads.

"Fine," the mother says.

I hand Joey the car and truck that sticks to my palm a bit from the sweat. He heads home with his mom. He hugs the Hot Wheels close to his chest. He turns back to wave to me one last time before they cross the street.

Try Being Grounded

. . .

I turn the key to my front door, expecting the same as any other night, for my father to be passed out cold on the sofa, only to wake around two a.m. for some kind of fix while I pretend I can't hear him.

But tonight, he's not yet passed out, so I'm in for a Treat.

A small box of period pads flies across the room, nearly missing my head.

"Your school called today," he grunts.

I bend to pick up the pads then stand up only to be hit in the temple by a box of tampons. It hurts, but I don't show it.

I'm not sure, in this moment, if Dr. Tandalay would encourage me to escape into my imagination or if this is when I'm supposed to ground myself with colors, or my five senses, or what.

I think hard about what I "see" — my father, familiarly under some kind of influence.

What do I "smell"? A mix of stale smoke, empty beer bottles and moldy wood panels.

How is this good for me again? Concentrate, Missy.

Okay, what do I "hear"?

"So what is your preference anyway? Slender? Long? Applicator? Nighttime?" Treat shouts.

I choose to ignore him. I know his question is rhetorical. He's baiting me. I head for the stairs like a salmon swims upstream. I want the solace of a different floor of the house, away from my father's wrath.

"Come back here, young lady," he demands. He emphasizes "young lady" like I'm a thorn in his side.

I'm not entirely sure what to do so I just stand there with my back to him. I have no measure of how intoxicated or impaired he is because I've been at the store all night. I have no idea of the lengths to which he will go to make me feel as bad, or worse, than him.

Dr. Tandalay would tell me to try something else. So I look for ... something red. The crimson Smirnoff label catches my eye.

How about blue? I see Absolut.

Okay, purple? The velvet bag from the king's Crown Royal is crumpled in a clump on the couch.

I give up and head for the stairs again.

"That's right. Keep walking, Missy. Leave me here to look like the bad guy who doesn't buy his daughter the things she needs.

Imagine my surprise to get a call from FACS ... oh no, wait a minute, that wasn't a surprise at all."

"I didn't tell them to call you," I say.

"Sure, sure."

"How could you have known I needed pads?" I try to bail him out. Truth is, it doesn't matter. My father forgot about me and my needs long, long ago. We don't even have food in the cupboards, let alone the toiletries that a teenaged girl needs. But here stands a man who is so wrapped up in his own warped perception of reality that whatever I muster is moot.

"You're right, Missy! How could I have known?" he puffs his chest, relieved of responsibility.

I approach the stairs, but stop when a rolled-up newspaper smashes the back of my head.

"Get a job, you lazy piece of shit!" he scolds.

That one stings, less so because of the blunt impact, more so because on some level, I know he's right — I should get a job. But getting a job would take me away from one of my only, if not my very only, pleasure in life: being content in Ren's company at the store.

But I just go with it. "Okay," I say.

"What did you say to me?" Treat was anticipating a battle. My affirmation confuses him, angers him even.

"You know how hard life is for me?" he starts.

I know what's coming. I know he's about to spiral from anger into a puddle of tears. I'd prefer having things thrown at my head, to be honest. I'd prefer a good ol' fashioned hurl to my stomach, but he hasn't done that in about a year.

"I work all day!" he screams.

No, no he doesn't. He's forced to clock two hours a day in order to maintain his compensation benefits from the government.

"Then I come home and just want some peace and damn quiet, but I get bullshit calls from your school about a pity party for princess Missy." I think he's done, but then he goes on. "So I go get you what I think you need, but of course I don't really know, and why? Because you're never home! So that leaves me home all by myself having to sit here without you. Without your mom. Without ..."

But he can't finish the sentence. He falls into his moldy spot on the couch and cries. It's not a loud, relieving cry. It's a quiet, wimpy whimper that seems more like self-justification to grab whatever vice is closest to him. Right now, that happens to be a bong. He lights it up and takes a massive hit.

I creep up the stairs to the familiar sounds of his coughing.

He calls up after me, "And if you think we're doing something special for your birthday next month, you're sadly mistaken!"

Don't worry, Treat. Never in a million years would I think that again.

Cannonball

⋮

I let the therapy office's door slam behind me. I don't apologize. The receptionist looks up. He waves and smiles. I don't wave back. He places his notorious, blinged-out clipboard on the marble counter in front of him, expecting me to sign it, but I sit down in the waiting room chair farthest from him.

He clears his throat.

I clear mine.

"Sweetie, you need to sign in." He puts a pen on top of the papers that are clipped securely by the silver clasp.

From over here on my chair, I feel an irresistible urge to go grab his clipboard and hurl it across the room.

"Come on now." He encourages me like a trainer coercing a puppy to give way and heel.

"You know my name. Sign in for me," I order.

He laughs.

I don't.

His expression drops a bit. He's not used to this Me. This Me is a bitch. Usually she sits tight within my confines, but today? I don't know. Today ... I just ... I'd rather be anywhere else but here. It's all a farce. My life is a joke that everyone is in on, except me.

As if he can see something in my eyes, he jots down a note on the page and then puts everything off to the side. I'm suddenly overwhelmed by guilt. I want to retract this encounter and re-try my entrance, but ...

Dr. Tandalay is on time, of course. She opens her door as she says goodbye to some middle-aged woman with puffy eyes and fist-fuls of damp tissues. The woman switches gears amidst her new audience of the receptionist and me, perks up to bid the doctor a good afternoon, signs out and exits the office.

Dr. Tandalay takes one look at the receptionist's clipboard then glances at me, but not before she winks at her receptionist. And there it is, the inside joke at my expense; the acknowledgement of my rebellion, but the realization of its insignificance; probably some kind of psychological insight into my sick state of mind.

"Missy, would you like a glass of water?" Dr. Tandalay foregoes our usual pleasantries and damn it, the mere mention of water is Pavlov's bell. I want to say no, but my mouth is a desert and my sole survival depends on what this woman is offering me. It makes me mad. I want nothing from no one. I want to be alone. I want to just curl up and —

"Yes," I say.

She nods as if I just caved. She puts her hand on my shoulder as the receptionist fetches my drink. She stares into my eyes most uncomfortably.

I burst out crying.

My arms are folded at my chest. My face is now like the face of the woman who escaped this office earlier. Puffy. Red eyes. Except I don't have damp Kleenex in my hands. Nah, when I cry, I let it drain down my face — snot and all.

I stop my crying even before I get into Dr. Tandalay's opposing chair. I always choose this upholstered wingback seat over the leather couch. There's something about the idea of laying down in therapy that really bothers me. As if I'm not exposed enough in this confined room, with a highly educated woman probing me with uncomfortable questions and pushy suggestions. Then you want me to lie down? Nope.

"How do you feel now?" Dr. Tandalay asks me.

"These days, I just —"

"Not these days," she clarifies. "Right now. How do you feel after that good cry?"

Good cry? Now that's an oxymoron.

"I'm fine," I shrug.

"Not today, Missy. I'd like a real response, please," she is more stern than usual. I start to wonder if she's having a bad day or something. Does she have a family? She must. There's that portrait over there on her desk that ...

"Missy, come back to me. Look at me."

Eye contact is hard for me sometimes. There's something just as threatening as laying on that leather couch over there about maintaining eye contact with this woman. This is no staring contest. This is a war; invasion into my trenches when all I'm trying to do is keep warm.

"Missy, there are certain times during one's therapy when something significant happens and it is my privilege to unfold it," she says.

I look at her. I note her use of the word *privilege*. I am smart enough to know that she could have said job, or duty, or obligation, but she chose privilege. Now, because I know how brilliant this woman is — after reading her impeccable reputation on Google — I'm wondering if using that particular word was a conscious decision, because I would have shit all over her question had it contained any sort of negative connotation.

"Today is the first time, since I've been treating you, that you've cried," she rephrases.

"Treating me?" And there it is. And she knows it right away. But this time, she doesn't indulge me. I can't push this woman off track today. I'm off my game or something.

"Today is the first time I've seen you cry."

"So?"

"It's important."

What's so important about crying? What's this woman's deal? There's nothing important about some damn water spewing from the confines of my eyes. Big whoop. Water spews out of my crotch all the time and she never asks me about pee, does she? So what that I cried? I cry all the ... well, I cry when ... come to think of it, when was the last time I cried?

And then it's a cannonball to my chest. A pain starts in my upper left side and spreads like wildfire to all ends of me. I huddle over and try to take some deep breaths, but that makes it worse. I try short breaths, but damn it I can't get enough of them. Medium-sized breaths? I forget my rhythm. Short ones again. A wave of heat overcomes me. The room goes dark as Dr. Tandalay jumps up from her chair.

Absent Moms

$$\vdots$$

Yesterday's fainting spell crept up on me. Of course, it's not the first time I've had what they like to call an "anxiety attack," but it is the first time I full-out fainted. Dr. Tandalay went on about some kind of "biological reaction to emotional suppression," but the truth is, I probably just hadn't eaten enough that day. I would eat like a horse, but I'm at the mercy of a father who feeds me like a bird.

On my way across the cement, wire-fenced moat around Mom's penitentiary, I think about Dr. Tandalay's latest prescribed homework mission. I told her that I had no problem with my last task and said that I bought myself something really special. As I babbled on and on to her, seemingly drunk off my low blood pressure episode as oxygen struggled its way back into my brain, I turned the story of timid Joey and his layaway Hot Wheels into mighty Missy and her pink, paid-for, princess-cut, party dress.

Seriously. A dress? It's laughable. Not only do I not have a reservoir of cash to make such a purchase, I don't have the desire nor the need for a dress. But Dr. Tandalay bought the fabricated story. She seemed pleased enough — she even asked me to email her a pic of me in the dress.

Then she took my missions to the next level and told me to write a letter to myself.

"A letter about what?" I asked.

"Anything you like," she answered.

"It would be a very short letter. I don't like much," I joked.

She didn't laugh. "Write yourself a letter about something you might like, then. Or maybe something you have liked. Give yourself permission to express yourself creatively, like you used to enjoy doing."

How did she remember that? "Many people who have experienced trauma in their lives seek solace in the free form act of writing."

Trauma?

"Suspend your inhibitions, Missy, and just go with it, even if it feels unrealistic. Even if, maybe especially if, it feels risky to you." She tried to clarify; but I still sat there confused.

And I still am, obviously. Musings about this assignment highjack my thoughts all the way to the prison doors where I comply with the entrance drill and safety procedures. I'm always relieved about three things. One, they don't take my iPhone. Two, they don't find my recording thingy and three, they don't demand to check up my butt for drugs. I'd never in my life do something like that for my mother, or anyone for that matter, but with me and my lacking capacity for eye-contact, I always feel like they think I'm guilty of something.

I get in, without any threat to my anal cavity, and I see George is standing post in the visitation hall. He pretends he doesn't see me, but I catch the very corners of his full lips creep up slightly, threatening a smile, and it's enough for me. I know he'd release that smile if he could, but he can't. Acts of kindness render guards weak, and they can't have reputations as such.

I see Mom in her usual spot and when she looks up at me, I feel the very corners of my own lips creep up slightly, but when I note that hers are flatlined, I suppress my urge to smile deep, deep within me, and it burns the whole way down until my belly aches.

"Hi." I eventually sit across from her. We're allowed to hug. I know this because we did once, a few months back when Ms. FACS was here with me for her annual, obligatory co-visit, which definitely explained Mom's public display of affection.

"Hi," Mom says back. I reach out my hand to her, over the table, and she swats it away. "Don't do that. They'll think you're passing me something."

I retract my hand like a mousetrap snap. I tuck it on my lap. I look over at George. I don't think he would have thought that.

"Sit up straight," Mom orders.

"Wow," I say.

"Pardon?"

"Nothing."

"No. What? Say what you want to say, Missy," she pushes.

"I really don't have anything to say. I'm sorry. I was hoping for a nice visit today, that's all."

"Oh, that's all, is it? Just a quaint little catch up? No pressure, right? Now let me just sit here and ponder how I can re-phrase details of this hell-hole to appease you." She taps her forefinger on her chin and dramatically thinks aloud. "How can one describe the bland food, for example, so as not to disappoint you?"

Same as I would my ketchup sandwiches and mini tin cans of Coke.

"We can play hangman," I suggest.

"The irony is too real," she says, slaughtering my idea.

"I can ask George for a deck of cards," I try again, which isn't like me at all.

"Who is George?" Mom asks. This surprises me, but then I give my head a shake, remembering where I am. I'm sure there's no personal interactions between the guards and the inmates. I point to George.

Mom guffaws incredulously. "I don't feel like playing cards," she says.

"You play with the inmates," is my knee-jerk reaction and I wish instantly I could cash in a take-back.

She asks the question that burns my blood. "Are you getting your period?"

"Forget I asked," I say. "I'm sorry." I lower my head to wait out the awkward pause that follows until —

"How is your father?" she asks.

"Great." My voice is so high I imagine the jail's protective panels shatter to pieces.

"Has he been seeing anyone?" she wonders.

What? "No." I sit back in my chair to catch a sharp breath.

"I bet he is," she insists.

"I really don't think he —"

"I bet it's Carly. Has she ever come around, over the past year?"

"Dad doesn't leave the couch."

"Never?"

"I guess he works a couple hours a day, a few days a week," I say.

"To keep the government off his back." We both giggle a bit at the thought of the worker's compensation team and how desperately Dad tries to deter them, despite ourselves. Mom looks up at the clock. I notice.

"You can go," I give her an out.

"Okay," Mom accepts; my heart crumbles. "I do want to get some time in, in the gym." She raises her hand to get George's attention. He takes his time walking over.

Out of the corner of my eye, I see Luke walk in to the visitation hall. He isn't alone. Ms. FACS walks slightly ahead of him. The over-pronounced smile on her face mocks the room like Joker's grin.

They head up to a woman who I'm assuming is Luke's mother, just as she finishes pinching her cheeks in lieu of cosmetic blush. When the woman spots Luke and Priscilla, she sits up straight. There is a massive stain on the front of her green uniform. She's missing one of her front teeth. I question if maybe she's not Luke's mother. She doesn't have the same mysterious, black eyes. Maybe that's a gift from his father?

"Earth to Missy." Mom waves her hands in my face. I look up and George is standing behind her, waiting to escort her out of the visitation hall. I'm consumed with wonder about Luke and the goings-on behind me.

"Whatever." Mom dismisses me and turns to go with George.

He leads her through the alarmed door, but not before checking that another guard is standing post to cover his absence. George looks back to me and waves. My mother does not.

The woman stands once Luke and Priscilla are within distance. The new guard stiffens, but Ms. FACS motions for her to ease up. This irritates the guard who no doubt opposes Ms. FACS's assumption that everything is under control with the mere flick of her untrained hand.

I'm more sure the woman is Luke's mother because of their similar stature and profiles. Luke's mother goes in for a hug and Luke just stands there, hands still at his sides. His mother laughs uncomfortably, then side-punches his arm like an old mate at a seedy pub. The guard stations a little closer.

Ms. FACS sits across from Luke's mother. From what I can see, it seems they ask Luke to join them. He doesn't move.

"She's full of shit," he says, about his mother to Ms. FACS, loud enough for all of us to hear.

The mother's laugh heightens, like it's a cute joke. Ms. FACS fidgets and spins her massive earrings. Luke's mother says something I can't hear — I wish my table were closer — but Luke's response, on the other hand, is more than audible.

"She isn't even at the table when she's at the table, which is pretty much never. This is a waste of my time." The truth of his words sound bells to my soul.

Luke flips his mother the bird and salutes Ms. FACS before he turns to walk out.

Something, beyond the fact that I have to leave, propels me to follow him out.

Luke's Deal

⋮

I slip through the exit door before it slams behind Luke. My footsteps are light; he doesn't know I'm behind him. His hands are iron fists at his sides. His walk is menacing and heavy. He's working hard to catch his breath. I go to say something —

As Luke stops dead and lets out a sound quite unlike anything I've heard before. It's a fireball of pent-up energy that hurls itself from wall to wall to ceiling to floor, enveloping me in his rage.

Luke launches an assault of punches on the steel wall confines. His bare knuckles bleed surrender. He's relentless.

I clear my throat.

Luke startles to a halt. I'm sure he wonders who the hell is behind him, but he doesn't turn to me.

I don't know what to do next. So I do nothing.

Cleverly, Luke opts to look up into the circular mirror in the top corner of the hallway that prevents people from smashing into each other through the open-and-close doors. He meets my eyes in the reflection. He still doesn't turn to me.

"What are you doing here?" he manages through clenched teeth.

I clear my throat again. "I ... well ... I just ..."

"Spit it out, Bell."

He knows my last name?! Does he know my first name?

"It's just that ... it's hard to explain, but ..."

"Nothing is hard to explain," he states. "So either it's sad or it's a lie."

"Paleomagnetism is hard to explain," is the disappointing drivel that diarrheas from my mouth. I see a shift in Luke's eyes.

"Paleomagnetism is black balls with direction from the center of the earth," he deflects my crap.

"My mom is here, too," I breathe.

"Well doesn't that make us special?" The sarcasm drips from his pursed lips. "Move along, so I can get back to what I was doing."

"You move along, so I can get back to what I want to do." And where that came from, inside me, I have no idea.

Luke turns, walks right up to me and asks, "Do you think this is some kind of joke, Bell?"

I hold my ground. "Yeah. It's hilarious both our moms are assholes."

"Don't talk about my mother like that." He is right in my face now. I realize the distastefulness of my joke and am suddenly swamped with memories of my many insipid one-liners.

The sudden silence irks him.

"It's complicated," he grunts.

"Why don't you go back in there?" Part of me wants to pry

while a different part of me urges me to shut my damn mouth. "At least yours probably hasn't left the table."

"Why don't you mind your own business," he suggests.

"It's just, I never leave the table first," I say.

"Well la-di-da, Bell." He turns to go.

"I prefer to be called Missy."

Luke stops. He turns back around. "She's only sitting there because Priscilla is here. She doesn't want to see me. Bell."

"It's ... complicated," I retort.

Luke holds my gaze for a moment longer than I'd expect him to — much longer than I imagined I could ever hold his — then he turns and goes.

When the final exit door slams behind him and echoes through the corridor, I just stand there. I am dumbfounded. I should just show myself out. I've done enough. I've shot my mouth off and, in one fell swoop, pissed off a guy who's pretty much the only guy I've ever wanted to talk to. On top of all that, I've over-shared personal information that I normally keep under wraps.

What's worse? My feet aren't taking me out of here. They're like two tent pegs, holding me in place. Come on now body. It's time to go. But my mind is elsewhere. My mind is back in the visitation hall. My mind is with the woman in her stained shirt wanting to hear words whistle through the space of her missing tooth.

Why do I care and why is my mind swirling with an idea that I can't let up?

Now here ... here is where most people would know to leave well enough alone and go home.

But we all know I'm not most people.

Now I'm back in the visitation hall and lo and behold, Luke's mom is still in the same spot, engaged in conversation with Priscilla the Persistent. If I believed in signs, I'd see it as vindication for what I'm about to do.

I reach into my backpack to pull out an old Blue Jays cap and plunk it low on my head — the last thing I want is to be recognized in the spotlight from Priscilla's earrings. I feel around in my pocket to ensure that the voice recorder is still there and its record button is within reach.

I look over at the female guard whose name I've never known because in my mind, she's just George's substitute and I'm usually long gone by now. So if I'm going to do this, I've got to do it now. I eye the table directly beside Luke's mom's and head for it.

The guard eyes me curiously. Does she recognize me? She glances over at where my mom usually sits and then back at me. My face burns red and I look away. She walks towards me. I don't know where to go. I don't know what I will say.

Then George barrels through the door and approaches her, as she's approaching me.

"Carrie," George belts.

The guard re-directs her stride to him. She motions to me and says something to George. I'm suddenly proactive and I beat her to the punch.

"Excuse me," I interrupt. George has a look of great surprise on his face and I'm not sure if it's because I'm back in here or if it's because it's the first time, in the many months Mom's been here, that I've said a word to him.

"What's happening, Larry Bird?" he asks.

Oh I get it. I'm tall. And I'm white. I like it. I half-smile.

George belly-laughs. "I'll fetch your momma from her leg lifts," he proposes.

"Nah, it's not that," I say.

"If you're done visiting, you have to leave," Carrie chimes in.

George notices my discomfort and calls off Carrie. "I got post," he assures her. "Take a smoke break. I don't mind."

Carrie abandons protocol like a dog seeing a squirrel. She disappears from visitation hall.

"Thank you," I say to George.

"Don't thank me yet. I'm about to escort you to the exit," he admits. "Unless, of course, you can tell me why you're being so weird."

"I ... uh ... I have to do a biography," I start. "The assignment is to interview someone really interesting and then write up a two-pager on them. Two pages. Whew. That's a lot." A little deflection can't hurt.

Even though his skin is dark, I swear I see George blush.

"I'm flattered," he says. "But I'd have to wait until my break to answer your questions. Side convos forbidden. In fact, we been chatting too long."

Oh no, I've led him on.

"Guard! What the hell?!" A disgruntled woman, alone at her table, shouts out. "I been waiting my turn. What do you want from me, a green light?"

"My bad Rosa," he calls out to her. "Keep your britches on. My partner will be back in a minute." He looks back at me. "Maybe today ain't the best day for this." He pulls out the two-way radio that hangs from his pocket.

"Wait!" I say. "I —"

George holds up his forefinger to hush me as he's about to talk into his device.

"It's her I want to interview." I point to Luke's mom.

A voice crackles through the small speaker on his radio. "I'm here Georgie. What's up?"

George looks at me. He looks at Luke's mom. He looks at the floor, then responds to his partner. "Put out your ciggy. Need you at post."

After a very awkward pause —

"Don't get me wrong," I say to him. "I think you're really interesting too, I just —"

"Say no more, say no more. I have big shoulders. But ..." I can tell he's looking for my name.

"Missy," I say.

"But Missy ... that's Lizzayn. She's a bull. I don't know what you're up to, but ... she don't play well with others."

"Guard!" ol' Rosa yells.

"Pipe down, Rosalie!" Carrie returns from her bonus cigarette break. She stands guard, relieving George. "Thanks for that, buddy. I needed it. Why don't you take one yourself after you escort your baby momma back to her cell." They both laugh.

George turns from me and heads towards Rosa.

Defeated, I mutter obscenities at my own stupid liaison with hope.

George is about ten feet away when he looks back at me and Carrie. "Kid's got an assignment. All clear. Leave her be for a bit."

It takes me a moment to realize that my nosey little plan may actually work. With George about to leave and sidekick Carrie not privy to the details of "my assignment," I have free reign to do it.

Why am I doing this? Why am I so compelled by the banter between Luke's mom and Ms. FACS?

I approach their table as inconspicuously as I can, rendering all parts of me so unnaturally natural. My movement catches Luke's mom's attention, so she looks over at me, causing Priscilla to do the same. Pretending to be fascinated by something on my fingernail, I look down at it so that Priscilla sees the Blue Jay and not the hawk.

I guess it worked, because I'm not called out yet. A line of sweat dribbles down my vertebrae and I'm out of breath when I sit down at the table next to them.

All of my worry, all of my world, and all of my wonder dissipates once I'm attuned to their conversation. With a trembling Peter Pointer, I press the record button and lean over.

Under the Influence

⋮

When I used to write poetry and short stories, I would get lost for hours in my imagination, strolling through beautifully blatant bliss.

It's been such a long time since I was in a state like that. I wrote my last poem a couple of days before Jeremy died. I would come to think of this piece as an ironic precursor to my dreadful decision that would plague my life forever.

I entitled it, "Now That I'm Older" and it went like this:

> Being one through twelve,
> Not quite knowing myself,
> Now about to be a teen,
> And finally be seen.
> Wished away my days,

Never wanted to play,
Can't wait to break free,
A bigger world is out there for me.
So it's almost here,
My birthday is near,
No longer a toddler or pre —
I'll show them; they'll see.
They've treated me like a baby,
Always answered me with "maybe,"
My leash now lengthens some,
Look out World cuz here I come.

Reciting it now makes me cringe. I was the poster child for "portentous." To think that I went from having it all figured out at twelve, to having my world flipped on its head days later, makes my skin crawl.

Alas, here I am, holding my same favorite pencil I used back then, ready to create this letter to Luke, pretending to be his mom. There was just so much juice in the conversation between her and Priscilla. Juice that I think would fill Luke up, without me even having to sensationalize it. Her take on his dad, the depth of her apologetic view of the past, all of it could be what that guy needs to hear. Sure, I could just play back the recording for him, but hello? That would be social suicide. So this will be ... historical fiction, I guess?

I hush the perpetual dings of my motives. Who cares? Dr. Tandalay is dreaming if she thinks I could ever write a kind letter to myself, but I believe that the intentions behind this composition are better than her homework assignment.

Even though I'm a leftie, I'm using my right hand. I don't know how else to make the handwriting look unlike my own, in case Luke ever sees what my handwriting looks like. Then again, if Luke was ever exposed to his mom's penmanship, he'd see right through this. What should I do?

I look over at my old, poor excuse for a desktop computer, crack my knuckles and dig in.

Interrupting my feverish keyboard strokes, the downstairs door slams shut and reverberates up through my old, single-paned bedroom window. I shudder; I can tell by the elaborate noises that follow that it's not Trick who returned home, it's Treat. If I have any luck at all, hopefully he will just fall asleep from his drunkenness into his spot, on his couch, for a few hours.

I need to concentrate.

I think hard about how I should word the ending of this letter. It's definitely the most challenging part. Aside from having no idea how Lizzayn communicates with Luke, no one has overtly expressed love to me in my life so I'm afraid I may make this sound too Hollywood. I mean, Lizzayn must love her son, right? I've always supposed that all moms love their kids and they just have unique ways of showing it, or don't know how to show it. I get lost in thought, searching down memory lane for ways that my mom hinted at her love for me.

Fists bang my bedroom door.

I choose to ignore them.

Treat rattles my locked doorknob. "Open it!" he yells. His words are slurred.

I'm frantic. I struggle to remember how to save a document that isn't done on Google.

"Open up or I break in!" he yells. I hear him stomp backwards — he's going to kick the door in. I rush to it and open it just as his foot thrusts forward, blasting hard into my solar plexus, taking my breath away. We both fly into my room and fall.

He bursts out laughing.

I can't laugh. Not only do I not find it funny, I'm straining to get a breath in.

Treat struggles to sit up and farts. He laughs louder than ever. He rolls over in hysterics until his head is next to mine. The piercing pitches and snorts blast my ear drum, but I can't move away.

"What's the matter with you?" He's pissed that I'm not in on the joke.

I try to talk, but air won't pass through. Water spills from the corners of my eyes.

"Someone's raining on her daddy's parade," Treat tries to wipe up my tears, but misses and hits my nose. "Bonk!" He giggles. "Get up!"

I know I'm not going to die. Simple biology would suggest that the wind was just knocked out of me, but holy hell, I feel like I will never breathe again.

Treat takes what seems like forever to get to his feet. He kicks the side of my leg, "Teenage drama. Get up."

But I can't. I hold my stomach and try to say I need a minute. Before I know it, he's on top of me, pinning me down. "Okay then, you asked for it."

His breath reeks of alcohol, pot, and cigarettes and I want to die. It gets worse as he gathers a mouthful of spit and talks through it. "This'll get you up." He laughs then proceeds to release a long, thick, whitish-yellow hork and dangles it over my forehead.

I gag. He sucks the spit back and then laughs even harder than before. He waits for me to get up. I try to muster the strength, but I'm still getting my breath back, which is even harder to do now under his weight.

"No? Okay then." He lets the wet mucus loose again. The saliva stretches even closer to my skin. I close my eyes and thrash my head from side to side. Sounds assemble deep inside me. An eruption is coming.

But Treat sucks it back and rolls off me. "You're no fun," he comments.

I work to breathe normally now and I just hope that he goes away. It appears my wish has been granted as he eventually staggers to his feet and heads for the door. He stops at the sight of my computer screen. He leans in to focus on it.

"Get away from there," I manage.

He giggles as he fumbles around with the mouse. "You writing again?"

I throw a hanger at the back of his head. "I said get away from there!"

He ignores the hanger. He scrolls through my business.

"What's this?" he asks.

I wobble to get to him, hunched, and try to grab the mouse, but Treat throws a hand up to hold me back at arm's distance. He's abnormally strong when under influences, like an ape. I fight to get closer, but I cannot. I try to bite him. He shoves me across the room.

"What the hell's the matter with you? You some kind of wild animal?" he hollers.

I get back up and brace myself for more. I run full-fledged at him and he clotheslines me. I fall backwards and he catches me before I hit the ground, then tosses me out of my bedroom and locks my door.

He wheezes in laughter. "Don't mess with this MMA master, you little brat."

I bang on the door. "Open it!" I yell. "That's my private stuff. You have no right —"

"I pay the bills around here. Get a job, then you can call things yours!" he says. All goes quiet. He's reading the letter. "What the hell does this say?"

I yank and pull on the knob, but can't open it. I back myself up then take a run for my door but only end up hurting my shoulder.

From inside, Treat complains, "Who taught you how to write? Goddamn teachers don't know anything anymore!" His words slur more than ever.

I run to the bathroom and search for a bobby pin to pick the lock with. I hear Treat laughing non-stop in my room.

I look in the third drawer and move things around. I dig deep into the corners and find one!

I run back to my room and put the ends of the bobby pin into the hole of the doorknob. I wiggle it all around and back and forth. Just as the lock clicks free, there's a thud inside my room.

I open the door to see Treat passed out on my floor, probably from a ruthless blood-alcohol level. I stomp on his wrist to free the computer mouse and he doesn't flinch. I kick the side of his ribs. He laughs mid-snore.

I'm left here to wonder how far he read, what he thought, and whether or not he'll remember it all come sober o'clock.

To Trust or Not to Trust

⋮

I've managed to slip into the school office's back supply room without notice. Imagine that! I look around to see if anyone is watching me before I take out all of the pads stuffed in my pockets and up my sleeves. I didn't need all of these and I'd like to replenish the ones I borrowed. I'm sure someone else will need these one day and they're a hell of a lot thinner than the monstrosities the school has on reserve.

I slip out of the room and my principal, Mr. Mianni, bumps into me. The stack of papers that were in his hands are now all over the floor. We bend to pick them up at the same time and my thick forehead smashes into his nose. He starts to bleed all down his lips and chin, and it drips onto his crisp, white, collared shirt. I rush to get him a tissue and accidentally knee him in the balls. I back away slowly as a train of *sorrys* spew from my mouth.

"It's fine," Mr. Mianni says, while plugging his nose. His secretary flies over with the rest of the tissue box. She doesn't knee him in the balls. I notice his fly is down. Now probably isn't the best time to tell him. I think my work here is done, so I excuse myself from the situation and turn to go, only to be greeted by —

A slow clap from Luke, who is sitting on the bench in the office. He gives me a standing ovation for my performance.

"Whatever," I mutter as I walk past him.

"What do you do for an encore, Bell?" he laughs.

"It's Missy!"

I scurry into the hallway and just miss Miss Maalouf. She flies backwards into her mop bucket and it sloshes a puddle onto the floor.

"I'm so sorry," I gush, but I keep going. I'm a walking disaster.

"Slow down!" Luke shouts after me. "Trying to set the school on fire with the friction from your feet?"

I'm compelled to sign him my middle finger, but I don't want to give him the satisfaction. I walk faster. I feel the inside of my jeans pocket to make sure a folded paper is in there.

It is.

It's the fruit of my labor; the letter manufactured from the intimate details I gathered from Luke's mom, two long weeks ago now. Pretending to be her while writing the letter was hard enough. Giving it to Luke, on the other hand, has taken me many days of courage and I'm still not sure I ever can, or ever will, do it.

Luke's hand grasps my shoulder. He tries to spin me around but I'm too strong.

"I didn't give you permission to touch me," I say.

Luke laughs.

"Don't do it again."

But he does do it again, so I grab hold of his hand and twist his arm. He yelps.

"Uncle!" He can barely say the word.

"What the hell is that supposed to mean?" I ask.

"It means I give. I give!" He begs me to let go. His arm's about to break loose from its socket.

"You give?" I press.

Luke rips back his arm to free it from my grip. I half expect him to dropkick me, but he doesn't. He just fixes his jacket.

We exchange glances. Once I'm completely sure he won't retaliate, I turn and walk away. I'm well aware that my actions could be perceived as harsh; however, in light of what happened two days ago in gym class, I'm not exactly a fan of Luke Geurtin.

Normally I like gym because I'm a wallflower. It's the easiest credit in the world. No classmate ever wants to be near me. No teachers ever push me. I don't know why they don't, but they don't. It's like teachers have some unspoken code for certain kids. It's like they know which ones may bite their heads off if you ask them to do a push-up.

So there I was, perfectly content in my all-girls phys. ed. section. I've been taking segregated gym all the way through high school. There are co-ed options, but why in the world would I willingly choose to sweat alongside members of the opposite sex? Gross.

Then my teacher went and ruined my life. She told us that "as a special treat" the boys would be joining us that class so that we could take advantage of the high ropes in the gym.

My blood boiled for so many reasons. One, because ... a treat? Every girl in this section chose to take the course without the boys. Every girl in this section surely didn't share the teacher's enthusiasm.

Two, I was annoyed because she insinuated that without the boys, we couldn't "take advantage" of the high ropes ourselves. This discredited our strength and skill.

Three, when Luke walked around the corner, it sealed the deal as the very worst phys. ed. idea, ever.

Faster than I could play the deadly-stomach-cramps card, the teacher told us to pair up. Dear gawd. Was she new with teenagers? Could she not have paired us herself? Could she perhaps have had a little empathy and at least ... I don't know ... euthanized me?

Of course, no one walked up to me. A small part of me thought for a millisecond that Luke might have chosen me. Then I remembered that our exchange at the penitentiary was pretty awful. Still drawn to him, the more I thought about it — which was a lot — the more I thought it might be because, being new, he knew absolutely nothing about my family's past ... nor what happened to Jeremy. Everyone and their brother knows about it in this hellhole of a small town.

After some awkward advances between the sexes, the peculiar pairing subsided. Only Luke and I were left there, standing alone ... together. He was too stubborn to ask me and I was hellbent on not asking him. The teacher stood before us and eyed up the situation. The struggle was real. Her pedagogical intuition predicted disaster, but upon searching the gym for any other options, Luke and I were volun-told to tackle the high ropes together.

Here's a real-life math scenario like the ones teachers are always asking us to do: take two students who suffered a great deal in their pasts, resulting in highly mistrusting personality types and restrain them with twenty-five-year-old ropes and harnesses for sixty minutes. Solve the probability of said students killing each other.

Luke's patience was the first to go. He tried to rush me through threading my harness straps, but I couldn't stop my hands from shaking. He said he'd do it for me and went in for the loop and I may have swatted his hand away harder than I needed to. The red welt indicated that perhaps, yes, I had.

Time was ticking and it was my turn to climb. I had just done a rather fine job supporting Luke's climb like we were taught to do. To protect him from falling, I learned how to belay — I passed the rope through this fulcrum thingy that caused enough friction to lower him slowly, instead of letting him crash to the ground like he kept yelling at me to make sure I didn't do. I may not have been perfect at it, and his journey back to earth may have been a turtle's pace, but he was unharmed. He wasn't shy about telling me how embarrassed he was by how slowly I lowered him, and he accused me of "holding him hostage mid-air."

When it was my turn, I glanced at the time and tried my best to think of excuses to play out the clock, but my damn teacher did one of those "announcements" where she pretended to talk to the whole group but I knew she was actually talking only to me and said, "Okay folks, make sure you get at least one climb in before time runs out because this is going on your report card."

Sure, sure.

Going up wasn't bad, actually. I had a knack for climbing and imagined myself an adorable koala in the amazing Australian Outback. I went all in and drifted off into La La Land, forgetting the gym, forgetting my fate was in the hands of Luke, forgetting myself.

Until the bell sounded.

"Hurry up!" Luke hollered. "I don't want to miss any of my lunch."

"Okay, okay. Just give me a sec so I can —"

But he let go!

I flew back — plummeting at a neck-breaking pace towards the ground until —

Yank!

Luke caught hold of the rope.

Whiplashed and halted mid-fall, I screamed, "What is your problem?!"

"I'm so sorry," Luke tried.

But I saw red. My legs went into frenzied kicks. I barely held back vomit.

"Get me down. NOW!"

Luke lowered me the last few feet. My feet touched ground and I wobbled to stand upright. Luke reached out to stabilize me and I threw down my harness and bolted away before he could.

And now here we are, a couple days later, the only two students in this hallway where we're not supposed to be, late for English.

"Where are you going?" he asks me.

"You know where I'm going," I say.

"What's she going to teach you that you don't already know?" he challenges.

I know his question is rhetorical, but I stop to think about it. What is she going to teach me that I don't already know? I read all of Shakespeare's plays years ago. I was a strange kid who read things beyond my years then composed my own monologues to see if I could hold my own with Willy.

"There it is," Luke says.

"There what is?" I ask.

"That look." He laughs.

What look? But I dare not ask. He's baiting me, and I'm late for class. We're late for class. I turn and pick up my pace.

"You wanna get out of here, Bell?"

I stop walking. I should keep going. I should just ignore Luke and put my one foot before the other and haul ass to class before she does attendance.

But I run my finger along the letter that's burning a hole in my pocket and I turn around.

Petty Theft

⋮

L uke leads me along a sidewalk. Neither of us talks. We just walk through the freshly fallen autumn foliage. I shuffle my feet, as usual.

I don't know what Luke is thinking. He sure is quiet. I concentrate on my pace so as not to clip his heels. I'm traditionally a fast walker, probably because I'm tall. Luke is almost the same height as me.

I don't like walking through this part of town. There's nothing wrong with it in itself. It's just ... it's the path I used to walk Jeremy to and from school. And being on this street reminds me of the very first time I tried that walk independently — a moment in time forever tarnished in my mind and heart. So I vowed to never take this way again, yet, here we are.

Luke laughs.

"What?" I bark.

"There's that look again."

"What look?"

Luke stops walking and turns to me. "I'm sorry about the other day," he says with a sincerity and thoughtfulness I never expected him capable of. "In gym."

I shrug, then deflect. "What look?"

"Did you hear what I said? I'm sorry about the other day."

"Cool. What look?" I press.

"You got problems, Bell," Luke assesses, then turns to continue walking.

Frustration builds inside of me. Why does he keep avoiding my question?

"Why do you keep avoiding my apology?" he asks me.

This seals the deal. This guy's got it all backwards and I can see that there's something about us that can't yield a normal conversation. It's exhausting. So I pivot to walk back to school. I survey the area for an alternate route.

"Where are you going?" Luke calls after me.

"Back to school!" My answer is louder than I meant for it to be.

"Don't be ridiculous. There's like," he looks at his iPhone, "twenty-five minutes left of class. Ten by the time you get there." He looks at my legs. "Twelve, maybe. There's no point now."

"Au contraire, my friend. There is a point."

"Au contraire, my friend?" Luke laughs. "You're so weird sometimes."

I used to think of it as wise beyond my years. An old soul.

"Yeah, so," I retort. Weak.

"Just ... chill out, would you?" he pleads. "Take that pound of chips off your damn shoulder and walk with me."

I'm not sure if it's the inherent truth in his words or his emphasis on "with" that convinces me, but class is practically over, so I shuffle alongside him.

We're quiet for only a very short time before I say it:

"What look?"

Luke ignores me and heads into a small convenience store. He kind of holds his hand out a bit behind him and I'm confused. Is that for me? Am I supposed to hold it? What the ...

I'm wrong. He just reaches into his back pocket to put his phone away. I blush the red of a Swedish Berry and thank the stars he didn't see my hand extend towards his.

Idiot. On all levels. I'm an idiot.

I stand in front of the store and look up at the sign. I remember this store from when I was little. I'm consumed by the memory and frozen in time.

I must have been five because Mom was pregnant with Jeremy and about to pop. I can still see the maternity dress she wore: blue stripes extended from the neck line and curved over her massive bump. Mom swayed a bit and clutched herself, telling me, rather loudly, that she wasn't feeling so hot. I figured that it was pregnancy stuff, which made sense to me. I'd probably feel sick too, if I got that fat in nine months. But it's my father who stands out the most in this memory, now that I think about it.

"Fill this prescription!" he hollered at the employee behind the counter.

Mom added, "What kind of pharmacy is this? To not help a woman in my condition!"

The cashier tried to keep control of the situation. "I'm sorry sir.

I'm sorry ma'am," she said. "This isn't a pharmacy, it's a corner —"

And at that point, I'm pretty sure my father grabbed the woman by the collar of her shirt. "Listen to me. Carly told us all about this place. Come through for us or we squeal."

Then my mom made obnoxious, dying pig noises. The woman behind the counter's eyes nearly popped out of their sockets on account of Dad's clutch that made its way around her neck.

I was terrified for the woman.

"Let her go," I cry out.

"What?" Luke laughs. He's holding the door open for me.

I'm startled back to reality. My memory vanishes.

"Let who go?" Luke asks. "You okay?"

I'm so confused. Memories aren't my thing. I have very few of them. Was that something that actually happened? I need to talk to Dr. Tandalay.

"Come inside," Luke says.

Before I follow him, I make myself a note about the memory in my ancient, mangled, cracked-screen, teeny iPhone.

Once I get inside the store, at first glance, I can't unsee my father's aggression. I turn my head away from the front counter that really hasn't changed much in more than a decade.

I spot Luke. He's in the snacks aisle. I mosey over. He hums and haws over the chip bags and does this thing where he touches each one he thinks about. When he gets to dill pickle, I hold my breath, hoping it's the winner. I love dill pickle chips and I'm starving. I assume he'll share with me because I don't have any money.

And apparently neither does he!

Luke slips the bag of chips into his shirt. Like a pro, he spins them to his back where his jacket is puffy and doesn't look suspicious.

"What are you doing?!" I'm not a good whisperer.

Luke eyes me a warning and it has *shut up* written all over it. "I'm hungry."

"Yeah so am I," I say. "But you don't see me shoving crap up my top!"

Luke whistles and pretends he's looking for a purchase. Other than the slight red of his cheeks, no doubt from a rush of adrenaline, he shows no sign of his disobedience.

Just as he finishes his Oscar-winning performance of a shopper who just can't decide, he heads towards the door.

My stomach hurts. Bad. Part of me doesn't know what to do, but another part of me —

"Put them away or I'll ... squeal," I say it loud enough and crystal clear.

Luke stares at me. He looks deep into my eyes and reads the expression on my face. I have no idea what I must look like, but be it what it may, he turns back for the chip aisle.

I walk out of the store and turn the opposite way we came. I'm going home.

Luke isn't far behind me.

And then he catches up.

"That'll be the last time I take you with me," he grunts.

I fake cry as sarcastically as I can.

"I'm hungry," he says.

"Boo hoo," I say back.

"You have no idea —"

"Oh, I have more than an idea, Luke. I am Hungry personified. But you know what I'm not? I'm not some loser who thinks the world owes me a favor. I'm not like you, Luke. When I'm hungry, it's my problem. Not theirs," I point to the store. "It's your problem," I tap his forehead. "Or your mother's!" Now I know I over-stepped.

But he doesn't react the way I think he's going to.

"What do you want me to do?" He motions to the urban landscape around us, "Pick berries? Arrow a wild boar? Grind me up some cattle?"

"Wait until you get home?" I suggest.

"There's nothing there," he says.

I relate.

He continues. "I'm short this week. I'm out of groceries."

He buys his own groceries?

"Yes, Bell. I buy my own groceries."

Did I say that out loud?

"I can read it all over your face."

I'm not one to be judgmental, and I realize I'm coming off that way. I soften a bit.

"I live on my own," Luke opens up.

Luke Meet Ren

:

When I step into Ren's store, with Luke on my heels, I feel different. I've walked into this place a million times since the day Jeremy died and I've always been somewhere on the Spectrum of Numb. At this moment though, there's this slight tingling in my toes and fingertips. I clench my fists and feet to try to suppress the sensations.

Ren starts to salute me but stops, midway, at the sight of Luke. Then he turns his attention back to his program.

Is he mad at me?

I smile huge at him and my unusual gesture seems to confuse him. It's like I'm on autopilot. I smile bigger yet and wave like a lunatic.

"Hi Renshu!" I shout. My voice cracks like a prepubescent boy and my face flares fiery red.

Ren isn't sure how to respond. His smile mimics my awkwardness and he nods. We both find comfort in ignoring the elephant in the room that is Luke. We carry on.

"You sure I can have anything?" Luke whispers to me.

He's referring to my promise that he can raid our tiny goodies section of retro candies and hard-to-find snacks.

"Yeah. It's cool. Anything," is what I say, but I hope like hell he doesn't pick anything too expensive.

"Great, because I think my stomach noises scared a kid on the sidewalk," Luke admits.

I watch him as he thoughtfully peruses the display, but he bypasses the chocolate bars and confections. He heads right to the bag of Lay's Bayberry Chips that Ren imported recently. "Now these look delicious," Luke comments.

Ren looks up. Almost smirks. Looks back down.

Luke motions to Ren. "So, what's the deal? Is that man ... a relative?"

"Does he look like a relative, Luke?"

"No, but ... stranger things. I don't know your story, Bell. Maybe you were adopted?"

Is that a question? Does he want to know more about me? Am I supposed to answer?

"Do you like these chips?" this query of his is real.

I shrug.

"I can't tell what you mean when you shrug, but I'm taking it as a no."

"I've never tried them," I say, while shrugging.

"Good. Me neither. Let's get these then."

A stupid smile creeps up on me.

"What?" he reacts.

Damn it. Worse yet, my brain can't deter the edges of my mouth from inching higher yet.

"Are you laughing at me?" Luke asks.

Inhibition shuts me down, pursed lips return.

Luke hits my arm. "I'm kidding."

"So, are you just going to get your dad back there to pay for this, or what?" We both laugh.

As Luke peruses the store and touches almost everything he looks at, I reach over to the small pile of Ren's Relics cards to grab one of them and a nearby pen. I scribble something just as Valkyrie skips down the steps from their upstairs apartment and hugs her father. She says something to him in Mandarin. On her way out of the store, she spots me, then she looks at Luke. She comes over and stands like she's waiting for an introduction or something. She'll be waiting for it all day if she doesn't pick up on my awkward cues to bugger off.

She gets it, eventually, but eyes the chips peeping out of Luke's joggers' pocket.

"You got a problem?" Luke jabs at her.

Valkyrie raises an eyebrow with an ease I find fascinating. She says more with that one gesture than I've said all week.

"You gonna pay for what you take?" she asks. And after a meaningful pause, "This time?"

This time?

Ren appears behind Valkyrie and taps her shoulder. He mutters some Mandarin and with a huff powerful enough to tip a pyramid, Valkyrie backs down then stomps out of the store.

Ren motions emphatically for us to convene at the front

counter. We follow him.

Luke whispers to me, "You're in trouble with Dad."

"Stop it," I say, and I mean it.

"Does he understand anything we are saying?" Luke wonders.

"Everything. Don't be rude."

Luke makes a face as if he never thought of it that way.

"She is super cute," Luke says, loud enough so Ren can hear him.

I stop dead. He thinks I'm cute?

But then I see Luke's eyes are fixated on college girl Valkyrie as she crosses the street outside.

I punch him in the stomach.

His *oooooof* spins Ren back around. Ren notes Luke's posture, nursing the blow from my still-clenched fist.

I smile a sarcastic smile that both Ren and I are much more used to, and Ren turns back around, knowing full well I'm in control of this situation.

"It was a joke, Bell." Luke can't stop laughing. "I mean, she is super cute, but I was just trying to get the man going."

I ignore him and meet Ren at the counter.

"Seriously, how do you know this guy?" Luke stands at the counter with me.

I hand the small card to Ren. He looks at it. It reads: I.O.U $6.77.

I was sure to include the tax. I know a lot of the conversions for popular prices by heart. I point to the chips in Luke's pocket.

Luke watches the symphony of knowing looks that Ren and I exchange. Ren takes the card and rips it into tiny bits. Then, he shoos us away.

Seems Renshu handles displays of affection with the same ineptitude as me.

I grab Luke's sleeve and yank him out.

"Thank you." Luke's words, directed at Ren, are way too loud, as if volume breaks through perceived language barriers. I roll my eyes and lead him outside.

We sit on a bus bench and Luke opens the chips. He takes particular care when easing the seal free, just enough to fit his hand into the hole to grab a bunch.

"Want some?" he offers.

I extend my hands. He tips the bag and overfills them. We sit quietly for a while, munching away.

I'm not sure what to do once the silence reaches discomfort for me. I don't know what he's thinking. I can't stop thinking about how quiet it is. Why aren't any cars going by? Why did the wind stop? Why do my Bayberry Chips chews echo like gongs? Why does he look so damn relaxed?

Ah, screw it!

I reach into my pocket to pull out the letter.

"So, I'm going to make a guess then," Luke says, out of nowhere.

I stuff the letter back into my pocket.

Luke gestures to offer more chips. I accept, but I don't know what he's talking about.

"He's ... a neighbor?" I realize that Luke is still hung up on Ren.

"Look," I start, "I came here once, a few years ago. And since then, I just ... kept coming back."

"Ah, so just a loyal customer?"

"Something like that," I say, hoping he lets it go.

"It's more than that," Luke infers. "There was some kind of voodoo crap you guys had going on by saying nothing. And, there's no way a guy's gonna give up free shit to us like that. We're punks."

"Speak for yourself," I say. Then after a while, "I had a hard time when I was a kid. This became kind of like a safe place for me." And just as fast as the personal reveal escapes me, sharp pains attack my chest. I feel light-headed.

Luke looks at me and studies my face. I can only imagine what I look like. I know I'm sweating. My breath restricts as I prepare for him to ask me what's wrong.

Except he doesn't.

A bus approaches. Luke squints at the driver and rolls up the chip bag. He stands up.

"Get up, Bell," he says.

I can barely breathe, let alone stand.

"I ... don't ... have ... bus fare," I muster.

A look overcomes Luke. It is warm, compassionate and patient.

I must be hallucinating.

As the bus stops for us, Luke's gentle hand grabs hold of mine and slowly helps me up.

"This one's on me," he says. He doesn't let go of me the whole way onto the bus.

Luke does some kind of secret handshake with the driver as we board without paying.

Touché.

The Beautiful People

⋮

The bus ride comes to an end for us at the mall.

The trip from the outskirts of our city to the downtown core is relatively short, which is partly good and partly bad.

Good because I didn't have too long to focus on how to fill our silence, and bad because it wasn't quite enough time to deter the impending panic attack. I can still sense its grip on the edges of my heart ... and invading the airways of my lungs.

"You okay?" Luke asks as he readies for the bus to come to a complete stop.

"I'm fine. Why?"

"You're the same color as my sneakers." His tone is more matter-of-fact than joking.

I glance at his worn-out, formerly white sneakers, stained a soft gray from dried-up mud.

"Let's get some air," he suggests.

❖

Mall air. Yuck.

But Luke was right. I feel better now that I'm up and moving around with him. Had you asked me if a trip to the mall would benefit me, at any moment up until this one, I'd have convinced you otherwise with an emphatic "hell no."

Something messes up the hair on my head.

It's Luke's palm.

Before I can say anything, he's inside an old-school media store.

What the heck was that? A noogie? Why would he ruffle my hair like that? He made it all staticky and fuzzy. I comb my fingers through to tame it some, then glance at my reflection in the glass partition of the store's entrance. I shrug, then head inside.

It takes me a second before I can find Luke, then I spot him in the aisle of old-fashioned CDs. I've seen hundreds of these things in my father's basement. It's funny I still think of it as "my father's basement," because that's what Mom used to call it. The three of us weren't really welcome down there because it was Dad's cave.

The three of us ...

I remember one time I tiptoed down there to look for some cardboard. I needed it for a class makerspace project and I had grand visions of building a condo for my favorite Barbie. Mom was distracted feeding Jeremy so I snuck down the stairs.

It was surprisingly warm, dark, kind of damp and smelled like skunk. I felt around and found a switch for the light. It illuminated a long table with tons of papers and junk on it. Leafy plants decorated the perimeter of the room. A pile of money spilled out and over a metal tray and I wondered if it were for groceries. A bunch of Dad's CDs were scattered, some covers open, some disks strewn. Just as I went to read some of their titles, Mom came crashing down and ripped me out of there so fast my neck sprained.

"You like that one?" Luke giggles.

I look down at the Nirvana *Nevermind* CD in my hands. The cover is of a naked baby boy submerged underwater, with an American one-dollar bill cast on a fishing hook before him. I don't even know why I picked this one up. Maybe my father had one like it?

I notice my thumb is right next to the kid's dangling penis. I try to suppress a blush, to no avail, and place the CD back with the other Nirvana ones, alphabetically. Luke reaches over my shoulder. I get a whiff of something. Cologne? Deodorant? I don't know, but I like it.

"Ever heard this one?" He's at the Ms row. I'm scared to death that he's going to grab the front one called *Like a Virgin* with a chick in a sexy, white lace corset on the cover. My imagination paints me a picture of my CD cover and calls it *Exactly a Virgin* with a pic of my noogied head. But he doesn't grab that one. He flips past it, not giving it a second thought, and pulls out a CD with an unsettling cover design. It has a kind of pale, skinny, white ... dude? ... with small boobs and a lumpy lower bit that looks like ... a faded jock cup? I know what a jock cup looks like because I thought it was hilarious when Jeremy had one for what turned out to be his only year of hockey.

The dude has gorgeous fire-red hair, mesmerizing yellow eyes and a bit of lipstick. Why is Luke showing me this one?

"It's Marilyn Manson," he says.

"Oh, so it's a girl?" I say.

"No, I don't think so. But really, what does it matter?" He takes hold of my hand before leading me to a listening station. Despite the incessant clocks around me reminding me what time it is, my brain decides to tango with my heart.

"You have to hear this song," Luke says as he inserts the disc into this demo player in the middle of the store. He hands me a pair of headphones that splits from a cord that is attached to his headphones, too.

Luke puts his headset on. I hold mine in my hand. I look around the store at the few customers who sift through rows of CDs, DVDs and vinyl records.

Luke re-directs my focus to my headphones and urges me to put them on with a motion of his hand.

"It's called "Beautiful People." It's nuts." His smile is infectious, but I hold mine back. He doesn't know how loud he is on account of the padded, massive ear coverings. I lift my finger to hush him, but he intercepts it. He takes my headset and plunks it on my head, messing up my hair, yet again. I smooth it and look around the store.

"You like it loud?" he shouts.

But before I can answer, the song kicks in and it's definitely loud.

"Turn it down a bit," I say, but Luke doesn't hear me. Not only are his eyes closed, but he has the same level of this ... instrumental assault in his ears.

The pulsing beat of the heavy song thunders through my core. I reverberate with the bass and I don't like it. I go to take the headphones off, but catch Luke in the corner of my eye. His whole posture relents to the song's animalistic rhythm and he taps anything within reach to the beat. His mouth does this little curl thing as he lip-syncs the words.

And the words seem to be about him not wanting me, him not needing me, and the cherry on top: him beating me down. Nice pick Luke.

Okay, whatever, I'm so over this. I'm just going to take these things off.

But Luke stops me. "Wait for it," he hollers. A few of the customers jump.

As more parts of his body start to move to the song, I just shake my head. I don't get it. Does he not see how many people are staring at him right now, myself included? I can hear it too and it's not worth my reaction.

Until the song takes hold of me in a way that is both confusing and empowering.

When the singer gasps the title of the song in a rush of energy that I feel in my toes.

I don't even know what Marilyn means or what they're trying to say, but I'm suddenly drawn to the intensity of it like it's an anthem of ... of I don't know what. And before I know it, my feet start to stomp.

Luke notices and I can tell by the shape of his mouth and the flicker in his eyes that he's egging me on with a *yeah* or something of the sort. I can't hear anything beyond the blazing notes and blasphemous lyrics.

Then the song builds to an intense tidal wave of rage, passion and permission. The double-dare from Marilyn Manson moves me.

We're suddenly kangaroos of teenage angst, hopping madly to the beat.

When Manson wails if I'm something beautiful or something free, I look over at Luke and let loose a smile.

We jump harder and we jump higher as the chorus propels us to new heights. We're practically on fire.

By the end of the song, we're a heaping mess of adolescent sweat and my heart beats in my ears. I can feel Luke's deep laugh through my headphones. He takes his headset off and hangs it in its holster. I take an extra moment before I do the same. The song's ringing remnants ripple on and although I know the reality of gawking customers awaits us, I want to relish this novel feeling of just ... not caring.

As I bring myself back to reality and surrender the headphones, I look over at Luke, who ejects the disk from the tray, pops it back into its case, looks around the store, then pops the CD into his jacket.

I react.

Luke catches my eye and freezes. He reaches for the CD and bursts out laughing.

"I'm kidding, Bell!" he waves over at the guy behind the cashier and the guy waves back. Luke leaves the CD on the player and takes my hand to lead me out of the store that I will probably remember forever.

As we walk through the mall, we don't say much. I know I'll have to tell him very soon that there's somewhere I need to be or I'll never make it to Dr. Tandalay's in time for my appointment, especially with all of the bus stops between here and there. Shoot. What if it's not the same bus driver? I don't have any money.

"What do you think?" Luke asks.

"Pardon?" I say.

Luke shakes his head. "Off somewhere again, Bell?"

I want to correct him on my name preference again. I don't

know why he's so damn stubborn, but a store's window display catches my eye and I know I need to go in real quick.

Can the Real Pink Dress
Please Stand Up?
⋮

The store is one that I'd never normally step foot in. Not entirely because it's not my style — even though that's part of it — but also because I could never afford its clothes.

"Will you please give me just a minute?" I ask Luke. "I'll be right out."

❖

Inside the dressing room of the store, the space is tight. There's a teeny corner seat that my arse could barely fit on and a couple of hooks. There are many signs warning of the consequences of shoplifting and not one mirror in here. It's so frustrating. It's like they pre-accuse us of something we probably wouldn't do, yet make us exit the private space in order to get a glance of ourselves, subject to the potential public ridicule of our reflected images.

Before I open my fitting room door, I think a second, third, fourth, and fifth thought on whether or not I want to exit, in this fancy, pink dress.

It's a spitting image of the dress that I fabricated for Dr. Tandalay's session. It's beyond pretty, but that's probably lost on me. I need a picture of me in it, like I promised her I already had. I tried holding my cracked iPhone at my full arm's length in this teeny space, but I couldn't get a full length shot. So, lord help me, I have to step out and ask a salesperson to take it. Thank gawd I had the foresight to leave Luke out in the hallway.

I open the change room door and —

Of course, Luke stands there instead. I've never wished a time-machine to swallow me up whole harder than I'm wishing for it now.

"Wow." Luke says the word with so little emotion that I can't tell if it's sarcasm or sincerity.

"Get out of here," I snap.

He smiles.

"Seriously Luke! This is a girls' clothing store. You shouldn't be in here." I'm one part angry and ninety-nine parts embarrassed.

"How disgustingly discriminatory of you, Bell. I'm disappointed," he jokes.

"It's Missy!" I shout.

"You buying that?" He addresses the dress.

"No."

"Oh, so the woman at the counter's your mom?" he jokes.

"No."

"Lemme guess ... I rubbed off on you. You're going to stuff it up the back of your sweatshirt!"

"No!" I hold out my phone. "I —"

"SnapChat this wish to your fairy godmother?"

"Stop it! I just need a picture of me in it! That's it! That's all I need. I don't need you to say anything. I don't need you to look at me. I don't need your smart-ass commentary, I —"

Luke grabs my phone from my hands. "I'm going to have to look at you if you want the pic to be centered."

An internal surge of blood starts at my toes and shoots up to my head. It's dizzying. How do I stand? Shoulders back? Gut in? Do I tilt my head? Seems to be the thing to do? And ... chin down? I think I read that somewhere.

"What's wrong with you?" Luke laughs. "Stand still." He steadies the phone on me. "Say cheese, Bell."

Mid-"Missy!" he snaps the pic. He takes a look at the resulting image and smiles. I go to grab my phone. He pulls it closer to him.

"Give me my phone!" I order.

"I will," he says.

"Now!" I shout.

Luke looks around the store to see how many people reacted to my volume. He laughs, but then his expression changes. "You know why I call you Bell, Bell?"

My audible sigh surrenders. I so wish this moment would just be done with already. "No. Enlighten me, Luke." The sarcasm spills from my mouth.

Luke walks super close to me. He untwists my entangled dress strap into proper form then looks deep into my eyes.

Is he going to kiss me?

"Because I'm part French and it's French for ..." He pauses.

My whisper finishes his sentence, "Beautiful." An urge leans me forward to kiss those fantastic lips of his until —

"What is that?" his words kill the moment.

I envision a massive booger hanging from my nose or something and I jump back.

But a booger would be the least of my worries right now. Rather, it's the small, crumpled white envelope on the fitting room floor, that spilled from my jeans pocket, with his name on it.

Before I can stop him, Luke bolts into the small space and grabs the envelope. "What is this?" he wonders.

I open my mouth to talk ... nothing comes out. I move my lips and tongue as thoughts try to rally into something ... anything comprehensible, but to no avail.

"It has my name on it. Is it for me?" he asks. "Is it from you?"

I shrug.

"Don't shrug, damn it. It's not a hard question. Is this for me? Am I supposed to read it or something?" I think he's about to open it —

"Wait!" My brain pulls through. "Let me explain."

He stops. He waits.

I say nothing.

He starts to walk away.

"It's from your mom."

Luke halts.

I hold back the vomit threatening to erupt from the pit of my stomach.

"My mom?" Luke isn't sure he heard that right, rightfully so.

I nod.

"This is a letter from my mom? Lizzayn Geurtin?"

"Yes," I barely whisper.

Luke is at a loss for words.

So I divulge, "When I was visiting my mom, I —"

"How long have you had this?"

Oh crap.

"Don't you dare shrug your shoulders, Missy. How long have you had this?"

Missy? Heart ... broken.

"About two weeks." I don't even know how he heard me. My words were so quiet.

Luke stares at me. The pain in his eyes strikes like daggers into mine.

I lean forward. "Luke, listen ... I ..."

Luke turns and walks away.

I follow him.

"Get away from me," he insists.

"I want to explain."

Luke twists back to me, "If you don't stop following me, I'm going to make a scene unlike anything your little brain could fathom."

He turns again and jogs, leaving the store.

"How am I going to get home?" I shout.

"On your fucking broomstick," Luke shouts back then weaves through the crowd of shoppers until he's out of my sight.

The rain pelts my head like a drum line of *I-told-you-so*s. I try to shield myself but it's coming at me from all directions.

I consider everything I can do right now, but the only plausible thing is to just ... walk. It's about a ninety-minute walk to Dr. Tandalay's, from here. That renders me too late. The only alternative is to hitchhike or something, but with my luck, I'd end up getting a ride from a Paul Bernardo-esque chaperone with an affinity for evil.

So I might as well redirect myself towards home. I lower my head and steam on.

A honk disrupts my misery. I wonder if I've crossed onto the road without the right-of-way or something, but I'm still on the sidewalk, minding my own business.

Honk, honk.

I look at the car of noise pollution and can't see the driver past the rhythmic sway of the windshield wipers. A hand sticks out the driver's side window and waves at me. I feel dumb because I don't know who it is and rather than stand there and look like more of an idiot, I maintain focus on my steps.

"Missy!" A woman sings, "Yoohoo, Missy!"

I recognize the voice vaguely. I narrow my vision on the head that is now sticking out the window, braving the rain, and I recognize Miss Maalouf. She doesn't look the same as she does at school now that she has her long, black hair down. Against her brown skin, her wide smile beams white, even under the overcast.

She waves me over. "Get in, crazy girl."

I make it over to her car. As I sit in the passenger seat, I turn to look at two toddlers in the back. One is still pretty small and sound asleep with his head flopped over his car seat chest harness. The other is a little cutie with her dark hair slicked back in a tight bun. She's wearing a tiny, peach-colored dance outfit. It's hard to say how old she is, young enough to still be in a car seat but old enough that it's just a booster.

"The baby is Krish," Miss Maalouf says. "He didn't have his afternoon nap, apparently. I'm fed up with that daycare."

"Why momma?" the little girl asks.

"And ears over there is Aahana, she just turned three so we're starting the dance lessons I promised her."

"Why momma?" Aahana asks again.

"Why what dearie?"

"Why are you fight up with our daycare?"

"Fed up, Aahana. Not fight up. Don't worry. Momma won't fight anyone." Miss Maalouf turns to me. "Yet," she whispers.

"I heard that, Momma."

"Shhhh, your brother's sleeping." Miss Maalouf looks at me. "Okay then, which way is home?"

"Oh, Miss Maalouf, it's really nice of you to offer but you're probably in a hurry to get Aahana to dance class and —"

"Nope. I'm early. Plus, it's pouring out there. Which way is home?"

I glance at her car's clock.

I look at her.

I point in the direction of Dr. Tandalay's office. "Can you please drive that way?"

As Miss Maalouf complies, without question, I feel little taps on the top of my head. I look into my visor mirror and see Aahana giggling away. I scratch my head an inch from her little fingers. She giggles some more. She taps me again. I scratch again. It goes on like this a few more times until she can barely contain herself back there, pleased her shenanigans are successful. She taps me again.

"Miss Maalouf?" I say. "Is there a spider on my head or something?"

Miss Maalouf looks over and realizes what's going on. "I don't know. I can't really see anything," and she turns back to focus on the road.

Another tap.

Scratch.

Giggle.

This continues for the rest of the ride, much to Aahana's delight ... and, strangely, to mine as well.

Check Up

⋮

Dr. Tandalay eyes the water as it drips from my hair. I wipe my hands against my equally wet jeans. I'm uncomfortable, but what else is new?

And of course, Dr. Tandalay probably won't start talking until I do so I'm just going to —

"Here is your prescription." She hands me a yellow piece of paper with chicken scratch on it. I always laugh when I hear teachers complain about a student's handwriting when some of the most brilliant people scribble unintelligibly.

I take the prescription and fold it up. I'm about to put it in my pocket then think better of it. The ink would run. I wouldn't be able to get my pills. I'd probably go insane. I'd probably end up in a straightjacket in some white-walled asylum where my only friends would be a tiny parade of ants carrying away my crumbs.

"Missy?"

"Pardon?"

"I said, I got a call from the cab company. You weren't at school for pick up. How did you get here?"

Using my Master of Deflection skills, I direct her attention to something more interesting, "I had a memory the other day."

I can tell that Dr. Tandalay isn't pleased that I ignored her question, but even she can't deny that this is important. "Tell me about it," she readies the pen in her hand and lifts the happy-faced clipboard.

"I'm guessing I was about five years old because my mom was huge, probably not far off of having …" I look down. "Anyway, my dad started strangling the woman and —"

"Your mother?"

"No, the woman at the counter."

"In your kitchen?"

"No." I get frustrated. I sigh and go quiet.

"You don't ever talk to me about your memories," Dr. Tandalay says.

That's because I don't ever have any.

"I'm sorry I interrupted your train of thought," Dr. Tandalay puts the clipboard and pen down. "Doctors get excited with progress."

I look up at her and I can tell that she means it. I relax a little. "We were at this sketchy store and all I really remember is my mom wheezing like a pig and clutching her stomach. My dad was at the front, yelling at the worker to get him something and when she didn't, he started strangling her, threatening to tell on her."

Dr. Tandalay waits.

"I think I yelled 'Let her go,' but I don't really remember."

"It's not important that you remember all the details so much as it's important to think about how you felt," Dr. Tandalay preps to take notes. She looks at me.

"Can we please change the subject?" I ask.

"You don't want to talk about how you felt?"

"I just want to talk about something else."

"Missy."

"No! Okay? I don't want to talk about how I felt."

Strangely, this seems to make Dr. Tandalay smile as she looks down at her clipboard.

Is she making fun of me?

She jots something down.

Out of nowhere, I blurt out, "Treat ... er .... my father really upset me the other day."

Dr. Tandalay lowers her head more and I'm pretty near positive I see the corners of her mouth curl up.

"Are you laughing at me?" I shout.

She looks up, straight-faced. "Absolutely not, Missy. I would never, ever laugh at you." She tilts her head all sympathetic and your-dog-died-like. "I'm just pleased that you're voicing some of your recent emotions. Did he hurt you?" she asks me.

"No." Now, of course, he did, but what's the point of telling her that part? I don't feel like a chat with Ms. FACS these days. "It's just ... he was all up in my business."

"Did you set boundaries? Like I taught you about?"

I start laughing, surprising both of us. It makes me mad. I stop.

"He may or may not ... remember ... something I did, that makes me very uncomfortable. I mean, he hasn't said anything about ...

this thing ... and he probably did forget because he was ... really tired ... but there's a small chance that he didn't forget and I'm having some trouble sleeping."

I add that last part because I remember that, in the past, when I told her I was having trouble sleeping, she gave me some extra medicine. I wait.

And wait.

"Can I have some of that other stuff that you gave me before? To help me sleep?"

Dr. Tandalay shakes her head no.

Fiery infuriation fuels this: "What good are you, then?"

Dr. Tandalay doesn't react how I expect her to. In fact, she doesn't react at all.

"That medicine won't help you sleep," she says.

"Yes, it will. It really helped me last time."

"That was different," she states.

"Nope. I was having trouble sleeping and you prescribed me something, then I started sleeping better. Same. Same problem. Same solution. Simple."

"You weren't sleeping then because of things that were out of your control, Missy." Dr. Tandalay holds her ground. "This time, it's you who is keeping you awake. I don't prescribe medication that takes You out of you."

What in holy hell is that supposed to mean?

I stare at her. She stares at me. I fold my arms and look up at the clock and prepare to watch the big hand tick its way around for the rest of the session. But she says, "I opened my email before you came in, since you were ... running a little late. Thank you for sending me that lovely picture of you in your pink dress."

I don't say anything.

Out of the corner of my eye, I see Dr. Tandalay reach for her phone and fumble around with it until I can tell that she's looking at the picture. "I love the material. Is that satin?"

I ignore her.

"I'm really glad you're doing all of your assignments with such dedication," she says.

I clear my throat.

"Who took the picture?" she asks.

I avoid her eyes.

"Missy? Who took the picture?"

"The saleslady," I blurt.

"Interesting," she says, "because when I zoom in a little and see a reflection in a mirror, there's a boy with your phone in his hands and —"

I swat her phone away and it lands face down on the carpet.

But she's not mad.

She's too busy jumping up from her chair because —

She sees I can't breathe.

It's suddenly too hot in here and the pains in my chest are ruthless ...

Trying to Keep It Together

⋮

It really hasn't been the best week, and with my birthday just around the corner, I'm more anxious than ever.

A lot of people look forward to their birthdays and I get it. They can be days of dedication, reflection, and joy pertaining to someone who is special. In my circumstance, my birthday is the anniversary of the day my brother died and then, a couple years later, the day my mother was taken to jail. So I'm pretty sure I've earned the extra chest pains and trouble breathing.

That all might seem like a poor excuse for me skipping class, yet here I sit on the toilet in the girls' washroom. I still have all of my clothes on, and I put about a million layers of toilet paper on the seat first. It's a weird thing how high school toilets don't have lids. I wonder why not for a while, to kill some time. I resolve myself to the idea that at least it's less work for Miss Maalouf. I've been in here for almost an hour. I just cannot bring myself to go to English class.

The bathroom's door opens, which is odd. This third-floor facility is almost never used, especially during class time.

Feet pace the length of the washroom and then I see a mop swipe smoothly side to side. I spin the toilet paper roll around a few times to pretend I'm just taking care of business. I wonder if it's Miss Maalouf out there. She's one of the three daytime caretakers at our massive school.

There's a knock on my stall door.

"Occupied," I announce in a somewhat disguised voice, just in case.

"Are you okay?" It is Miss Maalouf.

Another knock.

"All good," I mutter.

Her feet don't budge. She leans against my door.

"I know this may sound weird," she starts.

"Yep," I interrupt. "Can I please have some privacy?"

"You know you can talk to me, right?"

What?

"Missy?" she verifies.

Damn it.

"They were talking about you in the staff room. They said it's been three days that you've missed just this class."

I don't respond.

"Okay, I will go. But please come find me if you need anything." She starts to walk away, then stops. "Oh, and they're calling your parents, I think."

The bathroom door closes behind her and I'm left to think about how I'm going to handle this one.

My idea of handling something is open to interpretation. As I sit behind the counter with Ren, I am soothed by his intermittent giggles and sighs at his soap opera. The arrhythmic sounds keep me awake. It's late and I'm so tired, but I don't want to go home yet. I don't want to go home at all.

I think to occupy me, Ren mentions that something can be done. "The Beanie Babies section leaves much to be desired," he says. He's never one to sugar-coat things.

"Too stuffed?" If I had more energy, I'd have laughed at my pun.

"They look a little ... broken."

Broken?

"They're hunched over and lacking that certain something that would entice you to want one in your life."

Geeze, Renshu.

"I blame their lack of vertebrae," I stay put.

"Play God," he says. "Fix them."

Sheesh. Someone's in a bad mood.

Fine. I head over to the Beanie Babies and would you look at that. Ren's right. They look pathetic. Not only are they lacking composure, but the way their lowered eyes glisten from the track lighting looks like they've been crying.

It takes me a while to come up with something, but I find a bunch of hangers by the back door and carefully trim, bend, and shape them into question-marks that act as supports for the little guys. By the time I'm done, about thirty collectible Beanies stand at attention, showing off what's special about them, sure to convince everyone to love one.

Ren taps his hand on my shoulder in a very unexpected manner. He shows me the face of his analog watch with the subtlety of a neon light. He moseys back over to the cash register to finish counting the day's intake. I'm usually long gone by now. I watch his closing routine and I'm amazed by his speed. He counts coins with rapid flicks of his finger, never resorting to a calculator.

The store's front door opens and Valkyrie walks in. She locks the door behind her and flips the *Open* sign to *Closed*. She is surprised to see me. She barely waves at me then says hello to her father. Ren keeps counting, but manages a smile. When he's done, he says something to her in Mandarin. She looks at me. "You need a ride home?" she asks.

"No, thanks. I'm good," I say as I pack up my things.

Valkyrie heads to the back staircase to go up to their apartment, but Ren interrupts her with something insistent. Valkyrie huffs and turns to me once more, "It's late, Missy. Are you sure you're good to get home?"

"Yeah, yeah. Of course. I'll just ..." I hold up my phone. "Call my parents. They'll come get me."

Valkyrie says something to Ren — probably "I told you so." She heads upstairs.

I reach the front door and call over to Ren, "I'm going to go. Make sure you lock the door behind me."

Ren nods and smiles as he tabulates the till amount.

When I'm sure he's in the thick of his concentration, I unlock and open the store's door. I check back that Ren's head is down and, instead of walking out, I tiptoe over to the corner of the store where all of the vintage Lego sets are. Why someone would purchase a Lego set and not open the box and make the structure is beyond me. There's a space between the Lego stand and some Playmobil stuff where, amazingly, I can squeeze in and hide. I scrunch down and pull my knees in. I remember to turn my phone to silent and shield its glow.

I barely breathe as I watch Ren through two aisles. He writes down some figures then puts all of the money into a cloth bag. He walks over to the door and opens it to peek outside. I see him look from the left, to the right, and around a bit. A look of concern washes over him and I wonder what he sees out there.

After some time, he comes back in, closes and locks the door, turns off all of the lights then feels his way around in the dark until he bangs his shin into his apartment staircase.

Was that Mandarin for the f-word?

I wait a little bit before I get comfortable. It's going to be a long night and the cement floor will take its toll on me. As I outstretch my legs, an unexpected flash of that night, from almost three years ago, races through my mind.

To distract myself from going there, I grab my phone and am reminded that I have three voicemails. I dial in and wait to be prompted for my password which has always spelled "Ariel". My mom's favorite film was *The Little Mermaid* and it remains one of the few things I can recall enjoying with her. I remember humoring her by watching it the first time, but then the feisty mermaid's defiance of patriarchy and the sea resonated with me. I became a fan.

The first voicemail is a surprise. The woman whose name I can't hear advises me that I have a job interview at KFC tomorrow at 3:30 and to call if I can't make it. I barely remember applying for it. It was months ago. Oh great, that'll do wonders for my insomnia tonight.

The next message is from Ms. FACS. Her voice sounds even higher on the phone and it annoys me to the bone. She couldn't be more chipper with her fake concern for my well-being, wondering "if everything is all right." I hit seven to delete the rest of her same-old crap.

The last voicemail is Trick. "Hi, Missy. It's Dad. Where are you?" He pauses as if he's talking to me. Then, "Look, you're not in trouble, I just want to talk to you about school. You're usually home by now. Where are you?" He waits an irritatingly long time before he gives up and hangs up. I delete the message.

After some thought and trying this weird deep-breathing thing Dr. Tandalay once taught me, surprisingly, I fall fast asleep.

Bright lights and a vicious alarm assault my slumber. I jump up and hit my head on a shelf. A *Star Wars* Millennium Falcon Lego set crashes to the ground, spilling its insides.

Ren runs to the counter to silence the alarm as Treat stands bloodied by shards of the store window that, by the looks of it, he just busted through.

"Where the hell is she?" my father chases Ren and grabs him by the scruff of his neck just as a police car pulls up out front.

"Dad!" I yell. Treat, Ren, and now Valkyrie all whip around to see me. "I'm right here. Ren didn't know."

Treat throws Ren back. Valkyrie runs to her dad and comforts him with words I don't understand.

Two police officers charge in. "Mr. Lin?" one of them calls out.

Ren motions to them that he's okay. They all turn to look at my father who can barely stand straight. The second officer approaches him. "Tim, what's going on?" He points at all of the broken glass. "Did you do this?"

Treat looks at me over in the corner. His eyes well with tears. "I didn't know where she was," he slurs.

The officer approaches my father and pats him on the back. "This is a tough time of year for you, ain't it, Timmy?"

Like a switch, Treat rushes at me, yelling, "What the hell is the matter with you?"

The officer grabs him just before his fists hit me. The officer tries to be calming, but Treat rips retro action figures from the shelves and whips them at me. One of them strikes the side of my head and it stings so bad I think I lost an ear. I put a hand to my head then pull it back to study my palm; it's full of blood.

Ren darts towards my dad, but Valkyrie holds him back. She yells something at him and he settles down.

The police get Treat under control. He's handcuffed and taken to their cruiser.

I kick at some of the broken glass on the floor and turn to Ren and Valkyrie. My heart hurts with a million sorrys.

Ren says something, clearly shaken.

"Don't worry, it's okay," Valkyrie translates it.

The officer who knew my dad's name comes back in. "Melissa, we've got to take your dad in with us."

"I understand," I say.

"Mr. Lin, you'll need to come down to the station to make a statement," the officer advises.

Ren waves both of his hands as if to surrender. "I'm not coming in."

"You'll need to, to press charges," the officer clarifies.

"Like I said, I'm not coming in," Ren says as he grabs a broom.

Not all heroes wear capes.

"Well, that's your prerogative," the officer states. "Regardless, I'm taking him in for the night to let him ... sleep this off. Are you okay to get home, Melissa?"

My eyes plead to Valkyrie. She nods.

"Yeah, I'm good," I assure the officer.

Eventually, the cruiser peels away as my father shouts inebriated profanities at us through the window.

Not What I Was Expecting

⋮

Valkyrie drives me home along the quiet city streets. It's well after midnight but my eyes are wide open.

"I'm really sorry," I admit.

Valkyrie nods.

I wish she'd said something instead. The nod is ambiguous. Is she angry? Disappointed? Indifferent? Is she going to drive me into a river and be thankful I can't swim?

"That front window was very expensive," Valkyrie finally says. It's the most relief I've felt in weeks. I want her to tell me more. I want her to thrash me with how utterly disrespectful I was to stay there tonight without asking. I want her to remind me over and over and over how someone who considers herself to be a good friend to her dad would never have jeopardized his reputation and safety like that ... again.

But she says nothing else.

And it's so quiet.

How could I do that to Ren? How could I do that to my father? Who does things like that? What is wrong with me?

"Turn right," I say.

She signals and turns right. Her precision and perfect speed-to-rotation ratio is soothing and very ... Valkyrie.

"I have a job interview tomorrow ... er ... today, I guess it's today already," I stumble.

She makes very brief eye contact.

"It's the third house on the left," I say. "The one with the broken porch railing."

Valkyrie pulls to a gradual stop in front of my house.

"So maybe I will get that job and then I can pay your dad back for the damages," I offer.

Valkyrie nods. "Or your parents can —" She takes a closer look at our shack and thinks better of it. "Just let me know if you get the job. We'll work something out."

I'm not very good at thank-yous, so I just pause. I've seen it done in the movies and it seems to get the point across. I don't want to sit too long because it can be misconstrued as me wanting to say more, but I also don't want to get out too fast because it can come off as rude and unappreciative. I count three Mississippis in my head and then open my door. I get out. I close the door. Then Valkyrie drives off.

My street is dark. Only one of the five streetlights works fully; two flicker and the other two are dead. I stand in the middle of the street, because I can, and balance along the yellow line before turning towards my house.

I jump over the two broken stairs and land on the third one. It creaks in the quiet night and makes a neighborhood dog bark. I lift up an old, ragged rug that sits in front of my door and feel around for a key that ... isn't there.

"Damn it, Father," I mumble. I ponder what to do next. I walk over to the old bay window and eye the lower right panel. I guess it's a night for breaking glass, because I wrap the bottom of my shirt around my closed fist and go to bust through it but —

"What are you doing?"

I scream. I look to the end of my porch and see Luke.

Am I dreaming? I punch my belly like I used to do when I was a kid, to see if I'm actually awake.

"Why did you do that?" Luke asks.

"I was about to break open my window. I don't have a key," I said.

"Not that. Why did you punch yourself?"

"Luke, what are you doing here?" I confront him.

"You should be happy to see me," he snaps.

Happy?

"I should never talk to you again after that little stunt you pulled."

My stomach hurts, but I don't let it stop me. "Oh, please forgive me, oh perfect one." I lay it on much thicker than I should, given the part I played.

"Where's your dad?" Luke asks.

"What are you? A cop?"

"Seeing it's so late, I'm just wondering where —"

"How did you know where I live?" I say to change the subject.

"Everybody knows where everybody lives, really," Lawyer Luke declares.

"I don't know where you live," I contend.

"Do you want to?" He's facetious.

"Stop it, Luke. Seriously, it's almost two o'clock in the morning. What are you doing here?" I put my foot down.

Luke walks up to me and pauses. Then he takes a student card out of his wallet and slips it along the top of the window panel. He fidgets with it some more until we hear a click. "I'm just here to let you into your house. Your windows are old, but it would still cost a lot to replace a broken one."

I don't exactly know what to do once we're both in my house. He sits on my father's couch and kind of sinks in on his left side due to how worn it is. It's really weird for me to see anyone else sitting there.

A flash of Jeremy crosses my mind. He's little and jumping up and down in that same spot, snorting and laughing that silly laugh of his. I blink, and he's gone.

"I can't say I've ever forgiven anyone who hasn't even apologized, but here I am," Luke says. "I've thought about it a lot and I get it. You didn't know me very well, you didn't know my mother at all, and here she put you in such a weird situation," he waits.

My stomach turns.

"So, I'm saying I get it. I get why you waited so long to give me the letter," he finishes.

"You could have just told me that at school," I say.

"I haven't seen you at school. I mean, I've seen you from a distance, but you weren't in our class all week. I'm guessing you didn't want to run into me."

I make this weird noise that I wanted to sound like "that's not it at all," but instead it sounded like my mouth farted.

"I just don't really like that class anymore," I attempt.

"Nobody likes any of the classes, Missy. But it doesn't work that way."

"Is this a lecture or ...? I'm pretty tired," I say.

"I need your help," Luke blurts.

There's something about his words that tug on my heartstrings. I try to hide it, and I want to say something sassy or clever or flippant, but I say nothing at all.

Luke takes the letter out of his pocket. "Can you please read it to me?"

I don't take it. "You can't read?" I ask.

"Why are you so rude sometimes? Of course I can read," he hollers. "Do you know how hard this is for me? Admitting to you that I tried and tried and tried but just can't bring myself to open the damn thing? That I want to read it more than anything in the world but I freeze every time I go to tear it open? Is that what you want to hear while you sit there with those damn doe eyes of yours and stare at me like I'm some weak-ass baby?" He throws the letter to the floor, then darts through my kitchen and out into the backyard, where the motion-sensor light flicks on.

I'm dumbfounded. It takes me a while before I pick up the letter and follow him out back.

Luke seems relatively calm, but he's on the lawn with his head in his hands. If he's crying, I'm out of here.

He looks up at me. He's not crying.

I sit on the ground beside him and I start to open the letter. Luke leans back and lays down on the grass with his arms over his eyes. He braces himself with bated breath.

My stomach somersaults inside me. My intestines play double-dutch. My lungs collapse with each breath. I'm not doing well, to say the least, but I must hold it together.

I finish opening the letter I wrote and clear my throat what seems like two thousand times before I finally start.

"Luke —"

Luke chokes in dismay.

"What?" I ask.

"She never calls me that. I don't know what the hell I'm doing right now," he starts to get up in visible defeat.

I flash back to the conversation between Lizzayn and Priscilla. I distinctly remember being taken aback when rather than "Luke," Lizzayn referred to him as her —

"Lion," I correct myself.

Luke looks up.

"I said Luke accidentally. I'm nervous, okay? But Lion. It says Lion."

Luke hesitates, but then eventually falls back into place on the lawn.

I exhale and almost pass out, but I inhale enough to carry on: *"I know you have a lot of things you want to say to me. But I don't think you know how much I want to say to you. This place did a exercise where we sit and think about the one person that we want to say important things to and all I could think about was you and me. When I found out that I was pregnant with you, my boyfriend wasn't even in the picture anymore, he left me at the advice of his ancestors —"*

"She still can't even call him my father." Luke interrupts.

"Do you know him?" I pry.

"Back to the letter," Luke says.

"Sometimes I wish I didn't know my father," I blurt.

"Not only is that a terribly insensitive thing to say right now, it isn't your turn Missy." Luke speaks hard truths.

I go on. *"I didn't have help from my mom and dad because they were both hurting. They only had wine and beer and vodka to fix them. So when I had you, I was just a kid myself, but I didn't want to give you away to some strangers that would change you. I know I didn't do a good job with you. I know I scared you with my friends that would come over and they were not the best people for you to be around —"*

"You don't say," Luke comments. "Between the drug addicts and the couch surfers, the felons and the half-naked ladies of the night, I didn't think she knew I existed."

"Do you want me to keep going ... or no?"

"Yes, I do," Luke says.

"With no education and no help and no job, I was having trouble getting you food and paying the bills. So I started doing things I shouldn't have did to make money. That meant I had to leave you at home alone a lot. And I don't think I was there for you like a mom should be."

Luke sits up.

"A mom is supposed to show love and read with her kids and hug them and make them feel safe and I didn't do any of that."

Luke covers his eyes and starts breathing heavily.

"Should I stop?"

"No! Read!" he shouts.

Against my better judgment, I continue. *"It's not that I didn't want to do any of that. I always wanted to treat you better. I just didn't know how to —"*

"It's bullshit!" Luke stands up.

"I'm going to stop now." I fold up the letter as vomit pools in the back of my throat.

Luke freaks out. He pulls at his hair and paces the length of my backyard.

I instantly regret writing the letter. Should I tell him it was me?

"She can't talk to me, but she spills these things on paper?!" He's loud. It makes that damn dog bark again. A neighbor's light turns on. Luke isn't deterred. "What? She's just been, like, holding this shit in? Waiting until it's a prison assignment? Like, please write a short answer to address the lifelong pain of your messed-up child?" He's yelling now with panicked hyperventilation on the verge of a tearful breakdown. I know it. I've felt it.

"She's a liar. A liar then! A liar now! A liar my whole life!" Luke punches the side of my aluminum shed and buckles its side panel.

I step between his flying fist and the shed, catching the brunt of the blow with my shoulder.

"Move!" Luke yells.

I grab his hand.

He goes to throw a left and I grab that hand too. I am surprised by my strength. I hold his two fists and match his will to free them. His face is burning-red and sweaty. His black eyes are bullets.

"Calm down!" I say.

"Go to hell!" he yells.

He tries to pull his arms back, but I will not let go.

"Missy, let go of me! I'm telling you I cannot control myself right now!"

"Yes, you can!" I'm louder than he is. More neighborhood lights go on. "See something yellow!" the words fly out of my mouth.

"What the fuck?!"

"Yellow! Look for something yellow!"

"I'm not playing one of your stupid games! Let go of me!"

"Just look around for something goddamn yellow, would you?!"

Luke's eyes leave mine for a millisecond then glare back. "I won't! This is stupid!"

"My neighbor's upstairs light. You see it?"

His eyes shift to it, but he doesn't say anything.

"Now blue. What do you see that's blue?" I ask as he twists and pulls my arms, but I follow his quick glance at my house. "That's right. The gorgeous, wilting siding on my palace."

Luke's breathing shifts. It's less raging bull and more Doberman.

"Green. What do you see that's green?"

Luke's fists unclench and he lowers his arms. I still don't trust either of us enough to let go so I just hold his hands.

"Your poor excuse for a lawn," he breathes.

"That's right. You got it now." I model nice, deep breaths for him and whether he realizes it or not, his fall in line with mine. His whole demeanor softens.

"Pink. Look for something pink," I suggest.

Luke doesn't need to look hard for this one. He lowers his dark eyes and stares at my lips. I'm not sure what to do with my mouth now that his attention is on it. I don't feel like smiling, but I'm also not sad. I know I don't have the best resting face, but I don't know how to fix it. I look at his lips to try to copy their beauty and suddenly mine feel so dry and rough. I lick them instinctively.

"Can I kiss what I see?" Luke asks.

"Yes," I whisper.

Face It

⋮

I'm about as smooth as a cactus.

Don't get me wrong, last's night's kiss was as good as could be imagined. It was different from anything I'd ever expected. I thought it would be gross to smush my lips against a boy's. I thought I would gag at the inter-mixing of our spit. I thought I would recoil if a tongue ever dared graze mine.

But no. I don't know if it was because it was after two in the morning or because it was a full moon or because of the heat of the moment or the intensity of what was happening but the kiss was, in a word, fantastic.

I can't stop thinking about it.

But I also cannot face him! It's time to go to English class and although I promised myself that I'd attend today, that was before the incident and, let's be honest, I'm not the best at fulfilling self-promises.

The kiss isn't the reason I'm walking out of the school right now. The kiss would be a reason to walk right into my class, to grab Luke's face and do it all over again. However, I will probably never be in that position again on account of how the night ended. Dear gawd. It's like acid reflux of my soul when I recall what happened post lip-lock.

The thing is ...

I didn't know what to say.

I didn't know what to do.

I couldn't even think of some movie scene to emulate because my imagination abandoned me. As soon as the kiss ended, Luke went to say something ... and I will never know what he was going to say, because a flood of nonsense poured out of me that started like this:

"If you think you're going to get in my pants, you're dead wrong."

Stopping there would maybe have been forgivable. Carrying on, as I proceeded to do, demolished any possibility of redemption on account of this verbal diarrhea.

"Luke, I just let my guard down for a second and yeah, sure, it was nice for a minute and yeah sure, your spit tasted like Zoodles and I have an affinity for Zoodles because I ate a lot of them when I was little with crumbled crackers that soaked up the sauce so all in all it was pleasant and I was surprised by how soft your lips were because you seem so tough and maybe it's all just an act or maybe the kiss itself was just an act which makes more sense because you're just some guy and most guys just want one thing and it's sex and I've never had sex and I don't want to have sex with you or with anyone actually not even if Prince Eric were real which is saying a lot because he's hot with those big blue eyes of his so I never thought your black eyes would make me feel the same way and this is probably just some game to you to see if you can get the crazy anxious girl to let her walls down long enough to probably get her pregnant so she doesn't stand a chance at life and will probably end up an alcoholic drug addict like her dad or end up in the slammer like her mom, and your mom, in fact."

To no one's surprise, it didn't take Luke too long, after that, to just ... walk away, out of sight.

And then I went into my house and stumbled into my bed and tossed and turned all damn night.

So, not attending English class this afternoon seems like the most logical thing. I couldn't care less if Ms. FACS or Principal Mianni or Miss Maalouf or Dr. Tandalay gives me crap for it. Hell, add my father and Mom and Ren to that mix. They can all tackle me to the ground if they want to, but I will not set foot in that classroom if my life depends on it.

I figure a good four-mile stroll to the KFC should do to work off some of my embarrassment. This is my first job interview ever in my life. With Treat's threatening push for me to be employed and the looming cost of Ren's store window, I guess I'm glad I applied back when I saw the posting in my school hallway.

As I walk, I try to imagine what kinds of questions they are going to ask me. "Do you know how to operate a till?" Yes. I've watched Ren do it for almost three years. "Do you know how to give change?" Yes. Count up, like Ren always does. It's easiest and nearly fool-proof. "Do you know how to clean?" I will just fake that one.

I'm feeling strangely confident with my chances as I make my way to the fast-food restaurant for my 3:30 appointment.

KFC is half empty at this hour, but it's usually so busy. I head to the washroom first. I'm a bit sweaty from walking here and I need to freshen up.

I sniff my pits and react to the onion-esque stench. I palm a mound of soap from its dispenser and wash each pit, careful not to get my shirt wet.

I cup my breath to see if I can smell it, and I can, which isn't a good sign. In my desperation, I palm another mound of soap and just as I shove it in my mouth, a woman comes into the bathroom.

She cringes.

I turn my head and swish the disgusting suds in, around and between my teeth then spit them out.

"Sorry," I apologize to the stranger, for some reason. She ignores me and heads into a stall.

I quickly finger-comb my hair to try to tame it then I tuck my shirt in.

I glance at my phone. It's 3:15 and I read somewhere that you should try to be fifteen minutes early for an interview. You should also try to wear something blue, but I don't have much blue. And you should picture the person who's interviewing you in their underwear. Umm, gross.

As I exit the bathroom and round the corner of a wall ...
SMASH!

Right into a little kid carrying a tray of food and drinks. The chicken burgers knock the Cokes, splashing brown blotches onto the crotch of my light jeans.

"Watch it, lady!" the kid starts crying. His mom shoots me a dirty look before she heads back to the counter with him as I try desperately to wipe up the mess that's making a modern, misunderstood masterpiece of my middle.

As the lady complains to the manager and points at me emphatically, I wave and say, "I'm here for a 3:30 interview."

The manager adjusts her name tag and readies herself across from me at a small table near the entrance. I'm distracted by the people coming in and out of the restaurant, but I try to focus on the task at hand: getting this job.

I wonder why we're not in an office somewhere at the back. Maybe there isn't an office in fast-food restaurants. Maybe there's just the kitchen and probably a staff washroom tucked in the back or maybe they use the same bathroom that I just did and that's why there are signs all over the place teaching KFC employees to wash their hands really well.

"Melissa?" the manager says, rather loudly.

"Yes?" I ask.

"I asked how you found out about this posting."

"Oh, I'm sorry. I didn't hear you. I was just thinking about hand-washing." I'm unnecessarily honest.

"Hand-washing?" she asks. "What about it?"

"That you really do it, here." The thing is, I know how stupid I sound.

The manager glances down at my resumé and turns the one-pager over. "What kind of experience do you have in the food-service industry?"

"At school," I say.

"You took food and hospitality services at school?"

"Oh, no, I mean, I found out about the job posting at school," I clarify.

She just looks at me.

"I was answering your first question," I say.

"Can you answer my second question?" she asks.

I have to think for a second. "I do not have experience in food-service, no," I answer.

"That's okay. A lot of new staff don't. We have a really great paid-training program that could have you set up before you know it." There's kindness in her eyes, even though she can't help looking at the massive stain on my crotch now and again. "Here at KFC, stellar customer service and teamwork are highest in our mission statement. What do you think you bring to the table, on that front?"

I don't really get along with people, in general.

I've never made any team.

I'm traditionally more the complainer than the complainee.

My mouth starts moving, but nothing comes out until —

"I know how to work a till."

The manager blinks a few times.

"I also know that when one is giving back change, it's best to count up for accuracy and efficiency," I conclude.

"We have a computerized system, Melissa. It figures out the change for you," she says.

"Well, it might break down," I suppose.

"I've been here for sixteen years and it hasn't yet." She holds her smile as best she can.

"Climate change is ... getting worse and worse."

The manager shuffles uncomfortably in her seat. She jots something down on my resumé, the way Dr. Tandalay does, and starts to say, "Well, thank you for coming in —" she forgets my name and flips to the front again, "Melissa ... Bell? Oh, are you related to Timothy Bell?"

Ah, finally a question I know the right answer to yet I don't want to answer.

She waits.

"Yes. That's my father."

She thinks for a few moments to process something. When she looks up at me, her face softens even more than I thought possible. "Sometimes people just aren't sure how to answer these questions ..."

Yeah, that's probably it.

"Melissa, what good qualities would you bring to our team?" She appears to be giving me one more chance, for some reason.

I struggle to get air and feel dizzy. I tap my knees together rapidly, willing some blood to get its ass moving through my body. I take as deep breaths as I can muster.

"Why should I hire you?" She's re-phrased the question, as if that's the problem here.

I stare at her as I try to focus on a color.

"Melissa?"

"You shouldn't!" I shout. A few customers turn their heads. I stand up.

"Melissa —"

"You would be crazy to hire me. I don't know anything about food beyond ketchup sandwiches these days. I don't know how to talk to people unless I'm talking too much and making them want to disappear. I'll probably eat all of the food that's supposed to be for the customers and, more than likely, I wouldn't wash my hands as intricately as suggested in all those damn posters!"

I trip on my chair and struggle to balance. I fall forward onto a table, hit the edge of the tray on it, launch a pop into the air, and watch as it lands in the lap of —

The same kid I upset earlier.

"Get out of here!" his mother yells at me.

I jog to the door and just as I open it —

Luke is there.

Once the shock of our encounter wears off of both of us, his eyes lower to my Picasso pelvic area, and mine notice his somewhat dressy, blue get-up.

Before he has a chance to say anything to me, I run off.

From a distance, I can see that he's inside the restaurant shaking the hand of the manager.

Better than a Prince

...

For some kids, skipping school is easy. You just skip. No one really cares because you're not on their radar. However, when you're me, you get rabid dogs hot on your trail to get you back in class. A bunch of people who have to justify their jobs rally around you like they truly care when, in reality, you feel like you're just a checkmark on their to-do lists.

The office is quiet on this Wednesday. It's been seven school days since I attended English class. Despite many phone calls home and countless warnings from my father, I have managed to hold out. Alas, I now have a meeting scheduled with Ms. FACS.

As I wait on the office bench, I stare at the clock and hope with all my might that Ms. FACS is late so I get to miss English.

I fear defeat when I sense an adult walk into the office area, but it's just Miss Maalouf. Strangely, she's not in her typical blue caretaker uniform. She looks visibly upset as she tells the secretary she needs to talk with Mr. Mianni.

While Miss Maalouf waits and the secretary uses her phone to summon the man who is in an office sixteen feet away from her, she uses the back of her sleeve to wipe dust from the secretary's countertop. Her trained eye surveys the rest of the office then stops at me. Her expression changes and is on the brink of a smile, but Mr. Mianni kills the mood.

"Intisar, you wanted to see me?" he looks down at her.

Intisar. What a pretty name.

"I'd like to know where you get off changing my hours?" Miss Maalouf borders on insubordination with her harsh tone, and I like it.

"The budget for —"

"The budget? I have worked harder than any other —"

"It's not about how hard you work, Intisar, it's a matter of seniority." Mr. Mianni doesn't budge.

"I cannot believe how messed up this system is! Poor Alice has a wrist, knee, and back brace for crying out loud! She loves the quiet nights here. Yet you're forcing her to work days?" Miss Maalouf has an impressive way of being angry, but not emotional.

Mr. Mianni glances over at me then suggests to Miss Maalouf, "Perhaps we can go over this in my office. Can I get you a cup of coffee?"

Miss Maalouf has no choice but to follow him. "You know how hard this makes things on my personal life?" she asks him.

Soon they're out of my earshot, unfortunately. I would love to hear more.

It isn't long before I hear the clickety-clack of Ms. FACS's high heels.

❖

The guidance counsellor's office is small. I feel cramped in here with Ms. FACS. I motion to the scent-free environment poster on the wall and once she sees it, I ask, "Are you wearing perfume?"

She smiles at me, but ignores the question. "Missy, how can I help you integrate back into English class?"

Find me a time machine?

"I just don't think I'm learning anything in there, to be honest," I try.

"Now, that's silly. I'm sure you learn some things," she giggles. "What is it, truly, that's keeping you from that particular class?"

"I got my period in it and it went through my pants." I'm super proud of myself for thinking that one up so quickly.

"That's not the first time that's happened to you —"

Doh!

"And that was weeks ago," she counters.

"I don't really need English. I don't plan on talking to many people when I'm older," I half-joke.

Ms. FACS doesn't humor me as much as usual. "Look, Missy, I don't have time for games. I have another appointment soon. I'm going to give you some options here. Option One —"

"No."

"You haven't heard it."

"You're not going to get me to go back in there," I state.

"So, you're willing to fail the course? For whatever reason that you won't go in there, you're perfectly fine with losing the credit?"

"Yes," I say.

"You'll have to go to summer school!" she threatens.

I shrug.

"So, this is how it's going to be? You're willing to give up a month of your summer?"

"What is summer anyway? Warmer torment?"

"I'm going to have to talk to Mr. Mianni about it," she huffs.

"Okay," I say.

"Fine," she says as she gathers her things. "Go out to the bench. I'll tell him now, if you're absolutely sure."

"I'm absolutely sure!"

We storm out of the small room together and I plunk myself down on the bench as she continues on towards Mr. Mianni's office. Just as Miss Maalouf leaves it, Ms. FACS busts in and slams the door behind her.

I can see that Miss Maalouf's eyes are swollen and red. Part of me is terribly uncomfortable with the sight of it and wants to just hide, but the other part of me ...

"Are you okay?" I ask her. I think we're both shocked.

"I'm fine, sweetie," she says. We both know she doesn't mean it. She sits next to me.

"Listen," she starts, "I don't know if I will be seeing you as much around here. I'm on a new shift." She chokes up a bit.

"Okay," I say, which is better than me saying nothing, I think.

"You're a pretty special kid," she reveals.

For some reason, my chest tightens and I gasp for a breath.

"I've met a lot of kids over the years. I started caretaking schools when I was eighteen. There's just ... something about you."

I look at the floor and fidget my thumbs.

"I know you hear me. But do you *hear* me?" she asks.

I nod.

Miss Maalouf places her hand on my shoulder. "I'm going to keep checking in on you, you know." It strikes me as a promise, not a threat.

Miss Maalouf stands up. "I have to go work on making new arrangements for my kids. Take care, Missy."

After she leaves, I hold my breath and feel a strange rush to my brain. Then I manage a very deep breath. Its exhale is dramatic and a little painful.

"What's wrong?" I don't need look up to see who's talking to me. I know Luke's voice. He's standing next to the bench.

He sits next to me.

What's the deal with this damn bench?

"What do you want?" I ask, still not looking at him.

"I don't want anything," he says. "I have a session with our favorite cross-earring Family and Child Services worker.

I'm kind of shocked he shared that with me, but I don't react. Whatever.

"Actually, I want to say two things to you," he starts.

I sigh and look in the opposite direction.

"One, I got the job yesterday, which means maybe we'll be working together —"

"Nope," I say.

"Well, I'm sorry to hear that. I'll turn mine down if it means you can have the job," he offers.

"It won't make a difference. I blew it."

Luke laughs a bit.

"You find that funny?" I whip my head around and make eye contact.

His smile widens. "Yes. I can't explain why I do, I just do."

"Rude," I declare.

"Look, I don't know why you have to make things so difficult. I've been trying to —" He's interrupted by Mr. Mianni's door opening. We both look up to see him and Ms. FACS approach us.

Luke appears anxious for time, all of a sudden. He stands up. "Two ..." he begins, but it's not words that finish his sentence; it's a gesture. He opens his button-down to reveal his undershirt — it has a fingerpainted sentence on it that reads: 'Bell thinks I'm better than Prince Eric.'

My jaw drops. My cheeks heat up. As much as I try to fight it, a small smile escapes me.

"I've been wearing this flipping thing for days now. Where the hell you been, Bell?" he laughs.

My heart aches.

"Okay, Missy. You have your wish," Ms. FACS announces. She stands beside Mr. Mianni who has a grave look of disappointment on his face.

I ignore them and keep smiling at Luke and his stupid shirt. "What wish?" I play with Ms. FACS.

"About English," she huffs.

"What about English?" I ask.

"Missy, you just —"

"Speaking of English, I don't want to be late. I'd better skedaddle," I stand up and purposely brush softly against Luke before I excuse myself from the office and head to class.

Even from a distance, Ms. FACS's frustration is audible.

In Session

⋮

I think about Luke's shirt for the rest of the day. I was quite disappointed that he didn't make his way back up to English class. His check-in with Cross-Eared must have gone long. I wonder what kinds of things they talk about? Maybe since he lives on his own, she has a larger checklist to go over? Maybe he wanted to talk to her about the letter? Maybe he wanted to talk to her about me?

The cab I'm in pulls over to give way to a wailing fire truck and ambulance. I cover my ears from the piercing assault on my drums.

"Don't see that very often around here," the cab driver tries to make conversation. I make a noise to acknowledge him, but don't engage.

Once we arrive at Dr. Tandalay's office, I open the door only to be surprised by Trick, sitting all cleaned-up in a waiting room chair. I close the door slowly behind me.

"Come sit," he says as he pats the seat of the chair beside him.

"I ... I have to sign in first," I say as I try to walk over to the counter as normally as possible. I come face-to-face with the receptionist, whom I thought would be smirking at me, but is rather compassionate.

"I tried to call you," he whispers. "You didn't answer your phone."

I feel for my phone in my pocket. The stupid thing never rings since the last update.

"What's he doing here?" I whisper.

"Dr. Tandalay's request," the receptionist says as he hands me his sequin clipboard to sign in. I scribble fake-signature silliness on the line then look back at, and fake-smile at, Trick, who winks at me from his seat.

"I am not happy about this," I mouth to the receptionist. He looks from side to side as if he doesn't know what to do.

"All righty then, Missy, thanks for signing in," he practically shouts.

I go to sit by my father, but leave one chair between us.

"Come here, sweetie," he says. I haven't seen him look like this in a long time. I think he actually brushed his teeth. His shirt looks half-decent and I stare at him trying to figure out what looks different about his hair.

"Carly cut it for me," Trick says, as if reading my mind.

Oh, Carly. I see.

"And don't you be getting any ideas there, Missy," he warns. "It was just a haircut."

Sure, sure.

"The last thing I need is your mother thinking I'm talking to Carly," he says.

"But you are talking to Carly," I retort.

"It was a goddamn haircut." He slams his fist on the arm of his chair.

The receptionist looks up. "Dr. Tandalay will be right with you folks."

Trick clears his throat and sits up straight.

Then we both just stare at Dr. Tandalay's door.

Until it finally opens.

An old man makes his way slowly, painfully through the waiting room until there's enough space for my father and I to get to her door.

"Tim and Missy, good to see you. Please, come on in," Dr. Tandalay says as she holds her door open for us.

Trick smiles. "Hello Dr. Tandalay. Good to see you too."

I gag a little.

Dr. Tandalay closes the door behind us. "Sit wherever you're comfortable," she says.

I usually sit in the chair opposite Dr. Tandalay's, but my father steals it without consulting me first. I look around the room and there's only the couch or ... the floor.

I choose the floor.

Trick laughs. "Why are you sitting there, pumpkin?"

Pumpkin? I can't even.

Dr. Tandalay reads my expression. "Is that a term of endearment you use often, Tim?"

"I don't know what a term of endearment is, but that's a little nickname I have for her," Trick says.

Since when?

Dr. Tandalay studies my face. She throws me a rope. "Missy? How does it make you feel when he calls you that?"

I lock eyes with the doctor. I know she knows that I know what she knows. I shake my head no.

"'No' isn't a feeling, Missy," she says.

I look up at the clock. Dear gawd, I can't take fifty-five more minutes of this.

I serve a shot. "Do you like my father's new haircut, Dr. Tandalay?"

Trick laughs. "She's just trying to get me going," he explains.

"I'd like to apologize to Missy for a moment," Dr. Tandalay deflects. "Missy," she looks at me, "I'm sorry I didn't tell you that your father would be joining us today."

I fiddle with the carpet.

"She's talking to you, Missy." He kicks the side of my leg.

I move over so that I'm out of his range.

Dr. Tandalay says, "I had a feeling that if I did mention it, you —"

"That's not an apology," I blurt.

"She's pretty mouthy these —" My father can't finish his sentence because Dr. Tandalay silences him with her index finger.

"Oh?" Dr. Tandalay raises an eyebrow at me. "Why isn't it an apology?"

I take my time before I answer.

"An apology is a regretful acknowledgment of an offense or failure — emphasis on regretful. I think that your decision to not pre-warn me was self-serving and deliberate. Had you truly regretted it, you wouldn't have called us both into your office.

Therefore, I can't help but conclude that you are nowhere near sorry."

Dr. Tandalay smirks as she jots something down.

"See?" Trick pipes up. "This is what I'm talking about. This is what drives me to drink!" He turns to Dr. Tandalay, but talks about me. "Who does she think she is, talking like that?"

"A sixteen-year-old, perhaps?" Dr. Tandalay isn't fazed.

"Not yet," my father huffs.

"I called you in because I received a call from FACS about a recent incident at the toy store —"

"Oh, hell no! I'm not one bit sorry for busting in on that ... guy!" I know he held back a racial slur. Dr. Tandalay probably knows it too.

"That's not the only reason why you're here, Tim," Dr. Tandalay assures him. "You're here because I know that this time of year is an extremely hard time for you."

"Why does everybody keep saying that?" he shouts.

Dr. Tandalay sits up straighter. "People handle tragedies differently. Some people suffer many or most days, like your daughter ..."

What?

"But some people, like you and your wife, show patterns of being significantly more affected as ... anniversaries approach," she suggests.

I go to say something, but my father beats me to the punch.

"I don't know why I came here, Doc. You never know what you're talking about." He laughs. "To be honest, I thought it was one of our meetings about how it's going so I can access more support money."

Ah. His clean teeth make sense now.

"Not quite that time, Tim," she says as she flips through some notes. "Two years ago, just days before Jeremy's birthday, your wife ..." she looks at me and it's obvious she rephrases something for my benefit, "... involved herself with ... undesirable acquaintances. And around this time last year, when she was incarcerated for —"

Stealing me a Mac.

"That's all Susanna, not me!" Trick interrupts.

Dr. Tandalay flips a page. "True. You, Tim ... you were detained for a domestic disturbance on Jeremy's birthday, involving drugs, alcohol, and assault on a neighbor, who didn't press charges because he felt bad for you. Then on the anniversary of Jeremy's death —"

"We went over that! Susanna was arrested!"

"Not that one, the first anniversary, Tim. You were three times past the legal limit and drove your van into the graveyard, causing thirty thousand dollars in damage that the community decided to raise and cover for you."

My father's look could kill Dr. Tandalay.

She goes on, "That brings us to your behavior from the other night —"

"I didn't know where my kid was! I was upset!" Trick yells.

"You did know where she was, Tim. You went directly to where she was. You're using that as a crutch for your destructive actions."

My father stands up. "I'll pay him back for the goddamn window! Is that what this is about?"

"This is about whether or not you're going to be able to control yourself over the coming week. I'm afraid for your daughter's well-being."

"I'm fine," I chirp, silencing both of them. "I can handle myself."

No one knows what to say for a little while. I look up at the clock. My father sits, eventually.

"Tim, what are some healthy ways that you deal with any negative feelings?" Dr. Tandalay inquires.

"To be honest, I don't have any negative feelings these days," he replies.

Ever notice when people start a sentence with "to be honest," they're rarely being honest?

"So, you're telling me that you aren't experiencing negative thoughts these days?"

"He's numb," I mutter.

"Dumb?" Trick yells.

"She said 'numb,'" Dr. Tandalay says. "Can you expand on that, Missy?"

"He's always drunk or high," I almost whisper.

"She's a liar," he laughs.

"All he does is sit in Jeremy's ... his spot on the couch and down alcohol or smoke weed. Worse stuff too. I just don't know what it's called."

My father stands up. "I don't have to sit here and listen to this bullshit!"

"It's true, you don't have to. But I'm asking you to please sit down and listen to your daughter," Dr. Tandalay pleads.

He sits down.

I keep going. "We don't have any food. He spends all of the month's money on things to get him through, and I have ... nothing."

"She needs to get a job. Then she can buy the things she thinks she wants," Trick says.

"She is your responsibility until she's eighteen, Tim. Food is a necessity, not a want. It is part of your agreement that you will take care of her needs with the money you get from the government."

He laughs.

"I'm the one who makes annual recommendations to the Board pertaining to the amount of money you get and how those funds are allocated. I may have given you more control over the decisions than I should have. I may have overestimated you." Dr. Tandalay looks at my father, then starts to jot notes on her paperwork.

Trick puts his head down into his hands. Is ... is he crying?

Dr. Tandalay and I exchange glances.

I don't know what to say.

Dr. Tandalay doesn't seem to want to say anything just yet.

So, we let him cry.

And cry.

And cry some more.

After a while, I look up at the clock. Not much longer.

"I'm ... I'm sorry," my father says.

I put my head down. Dr. Tandalay looks up.

Through tears, my father manages, "It's so hard. I just ... I miss him so much ... it's because of me that —"

Because of you? Because of me.

"There's no time for blame, Tim. This is a time for healing and learning to deal with life and its punches. But right now, you don't have the arsenal to do it," Dr. Tandalay leans in for emphasis. "I'd like to see you much more than once a year. So I'm asking you again. Are you willing to consider that?"

My father is quiet for a very long time.

"Tim? What do you think?" Dr. Tandalay presses.

"Yes," my father responds.

"Yes, you will keep regular appointments with me?" Dr. Tandalay presses.

"Yes," he answers.

"I also have another recommendation that is a condition of a favorable report," Dr. Tandalay lowers her glasses and looks directly at him. "You need to take away at least one of your vices, and seek support for the others, immediately."

"Like AA?" he asks.

"AA is a great start," she says. She hands him a few pamphlets that she just happens to have ready.

He takes them and flips through them.

Why am I even here?

"Missy, you're just about sixteen. That affords you some legal empowerment that I would like you to read about." Dr. Tandalay hands me some paperwork. I scan key phrases: "Education is a Legal Requirement," "Youth Criminal Justice Act," paragraphs about "Leaving Home," "Civil Arrests, Domestic Altercation Information" ...

"Tim, this conditional recommendation to the Board is probational for a period of six months, at which point I will re-assess and submit another one. Annual reports are too spread out, given the circumstances and the FACS assessments I've received." Her tone softens. "I think what's most important here is that you have a daughter whose needs aren't being met."

"I know," my father lowers his head.

"Tim, look at me," she orders. He does. "I'm not just talking about food and shelter and ..." she looks me up and down, "clothing. I'm talking about guidance and support. I'm talking ... about love."

I feel a massive lump grow in my throat.

"I'm talking about soothing someone who was also affected by this tragedy. Melissa suffers in silence and isolation and that's perhaps the greatest tragedy of all," she states.

I wait in awe, for Trick to blast her, to jump out of his chair and damn her for her blatant inconsideration and minimization of Jeremy's death.

"Okay," my father says.

Okay? The lump in my throat is tenfold. I can't take it. I'm either going to puke or bawl my eyes out. I look up at the clock. Praise the lord, time's up.

I stand up and walk out of Dr. Tandalay's office.

My Birthday

:

In rare form, I decided not to go to the store last night. I'm hoping Ren understood. I needed a night alone, in my room, to think about all that's happened lately.

Here I am now. Wednesday morning. Incidentally, my birthday, and what do I have planned? A visit to see my mother behind bars.

I hear the front door slam. My father and I haven't really spoken since our visit to Dr. Tandalay's. It's been so intense and the air is thick. A kind of thick where we walk past each other and do this weird dance because we're not sure who should go which way so that we don't bump into each other. The kind where if one of us sneezes, the other actually says "bless you." The kind where if there were one Timbit left in the box, we'd both say "go ahead" and then be equally too timid to actually go ahead.

I know I should get out of bed for school — and I will — but right now, this is where I want to be. Horizontal and cozy in my blanket.

I hear footsteps up the staircase. My father is probably making his way up to his room after an all-nighter of some sort. I wonder if he's been at Carly's house?

There's a knock at my bedroom door.

"Yes?" I answer.

"Can I come in?" my father asks.

I don't know. Can you? is how a smartass would reply. I bite my tongue. "Yes," I say instead.

The door opens slowly. My father comes in and sits at the end of my bed. He has one hand behind his back. I hold back a smile. He's clean-shaven ... I haven't seen him clean-shaven in years.

"Happy Birthday," he announces.

A lump that has become all too familiar practically chokes me.

"Thank you," I manage.

He looks around my room. He stops for a moment at two little Hot Wheels cars that were once Jeremy's and shakes his head before his eyes meet mine again.

"Sixteen," he says. He nods as if he's talking to himself. "This is a big deal. Of course, we don't have your mother's truck anymore."

Was that some kind of joke?

He continues, "And I went and ruined our used van. There's pretty much zero chance of me affording a vehicle so no point in you getting your license. But ... I went out this morning, and got you this."

He hands me a white envelope. I can feel that it's mostly empty, so it's not a birthday card. I wonder, just for a minute, what he would have written, had it been a card.

"Open it," he presses.

A smile escapes me. I sit up and rest myself against my old headboard. It creaks and moans against my weight.

I'm notorious for taking my time with gifts. I've gotten so very, very few in my life, that I just need to revel in the moment, take it all in that someone put thought into me. It's the best feeling in the world. Much more meaningful and special than anything that could ever be in this envelope.

"Faster!" He's excited about whatever it is.

I open it.

Inside is a city transit monthly pass.

The lump in my throat expands and pushes with all its might.

"It's a bus pass!" my father exclaims.

I nod. I cannot talk. Silence is the flood gate at this point.

"You can use it unlimited. On any route. To get to wherever you want to go. Up to three towns over!"

We've hit that awkward moment of gifting protocol where I need to show my emotions the right amount to satisfy him. Where my expression and my words need to match his hopes and expectations. Where I should jump up and hug and kiss him for how thoughtful, unexpected and useful this gift really is.

But this is me we're talking about. And I don't know how to do all of that. I start to panic. My heart races and I feel sweaty. I have trouble catching my breath.

He stands up. I fear the worst.

"Don't cry," he says.

How does he know?

He walks over to me and kisses me on the forehead. "Happy Birthday, Pumpkin. There's Lucky Charms on the table. I'm going to go lay down for a bit."

He closes my door. I bury my head into my pillow and cry like a baby.

❖

As I sit in English class, it takes me a bit of time to get over the fact that Luke isn't here. I've been waiting for this class all day. He makes my mind and heart and body feel alive.

I tune out my teacher and her unoriginal thoughts on *The Great Gatsby* and just reflect on my birthday so far. The only eventful part, really, was the morning.

Just as I suspected, being sixteen doesn't feel any different, except for the episode with my father. That felt unique. After I finally stopped crying, I opted to write him a little letter that I left on the floor outside of his room:

> I'm sorry I didn't have these words this morning. I wasn't sure how to express what I was feeling or thinking. You surprised me, I'm sorry to say, because I'm not used to that side of you. That said, I was so happy to just have you there. The bus pass was a very sweet gift that I know cost you a lot of money. It showed me that you respect my growing independence and you're giving me a chance to spread my wings. That, or you just really want me to get a job.

I laugh again at my own joke. Then I added this at the end:

I hope this is the start of a new chapter for us.

When I left my house, I partook in the one birthday tradition I have. No, it has nothing to do with candles or cake or presents or a celebration. On the contrary, it involves me walking from my house, to the sidewalk, with my eyes closed. I can't bear to look at my driveway or where my mom's truck used to park. The memory is too real, on this day. I guess I'm like my mother and father: the pain of Jeremy is gut-wrenching on anniversaries. I'm still wondering why Dr. Tandalay suggested I'm any different. Maybe because I'm on inhibitor meds.

My ritual involved me leaving the confines of my house with my eyes closed. Voluntarily blind, I struggled to put my key in the doorknob hole to lock the house behind me. Then I counted my footsteps so that I didn't get swallowed by the broken stairs, like I did last year. I held what's left of a handrail as I lowered myself to the walkway. I took miniature steps, feeling for the difference of soft grass — from tough pavement — to stay on course. Despite my efforts, the gravel spots of the driveway still managed to make my stomach turn. I powered through the dreadful twenty-two steps and was then comforted by the new change in texture under my shoes; I'd reached the sidewalk.

"Missy?" the teacher asks.

Some people in class giggle.

"Yes?"

"I asked you why Gatsby is unable to put the past behind him?"

"I don't know," I state.

A couple more kids laugh at my honesty.

My teacher shushes them. "Come on now, Missy. I know you have thoughts."

I don't say anything.

My teacher does that thing where she's really talking to me, but she frames it as a class discussion. "You see, this is what I'm talking about. You guys are lazy. You're smart and you're insightful, but you're lazy. Your defiance is pretending to be dumb. It's disheartening —"

"It's not that he's unable to put the past behind him. It's that he doesn't want to," I blurt.

My teacher half-smiles. "Go on," she pushes.

"I think he's lucky, personally," I declare.

Her smile fades. "Well, that's not a very popular opinion."

"He draws on his picture-perfect, blissful past with Daisy in hopes that he can recreate it."

"But he can't. It's unrealistic. Had you read the book, you would have —"

"I did read the book. Personally, I'd rather live in an oblivious dream state pumped by positive memories than deal with the true crappiness of it. At least Gatsby is lucky and it's not the other way around. At least he didn't suffer an irreparable past that haunts him into submission," I say.

A couple of my classmates look down.

"The goal is to live in the moment," my teacher says.

"Says you," I retort.

A few kids chuckle.

My teacher calls on someone else who will no doubt give her an answer she likes better.

❖

As I arrive at the penitentiary for my visit with my mother, I walk in some kind of a daze. The kind where you are at one spot and then all of a sudden, you're at another, and you have no idea what happened in between.

I collect my thoughts outside of the door and take a deep breath before I —

The door opens and nearly hits me.

Luke exits the pen.

He shields his eyes from the sunlight and what was already a smile on his lips widens more at the sight of me. I feel myself blush.

Luke picks me up into his arms and spins me around two times. I feel so silly, but I go with it. It's like I'm on a merry-go-round.

Luke puts me down and wipes some hair out of my face. "Thank you," he says, and he plants a smooch on my lips. It's playful and loud and adorable. I smile a dorky, lopsided smile.

"I just had a good visit with my mom," he says. "Like, real good. Like, better than I've ever had."

"That's awesome," I say, but I can't help but feel a tinge of guilt in my belly.

"I just thought, all right, fine. The least I can do is be civil, after she wrote me that letter. So I gave her a slight benefit of the doubt. We didn't talk about anything deep, but ... we talked. She was so surprised to see me. You should have seen her face." He picks me up again and I have to stop myself from farting. I feel sick to my stomach with this weird mixture of happiness for him, but terror for myself.

"I really need to head inside," I say. "My mom is probably wondering where I am and stuff."

"Yeah, yeah. For sure." He puts me back down. "Go on."

I beeline for the door and he heads off towards the bus stop. Just as I step inside, I hear him yell, "And don't you dare think I forgot it's your birthday! I will come see you later!"

And the prison door closes.

The Candles Are Out

Even though my mother usually waits for me at one of the visitation tables, today I'm here first. I glance at the time through my cracked iPhone screen and I'm actually a little late.

I look around at the other people visiting. I see some small smiles here and there, but for the most part, visitors appear to do most of the talking while the prisoners sit and listen. I imagine they don't have much to talk about on account of their limited daily activities. I start to think of all the things I can say to my mom. The list is long, but I have a tendency to dwindle it to nothing. I'm going to try to fight that urge this visit.

If she ever comes out.

The massive armored door opens and George walks into the hall. He motions to the other guard to wait just a minute, then he walks over to me.

"Hey Bird. Your momma is tied up at the moment," he says.

"Oh ... should I go?" I ask.

"I think you can give it a bit longer. She be out soon, I'm guessing." He pats me on the shoulder. His massive hand feels warm and strong.

George walks over to relieve the other guard. They share some whispers before they part.

I start to wonder about Luke's plan to come to my house later. I didn't invite him. It's not that I don't want him there. It's just that, well, what if my father wants to do something special, like a birthday dinner or something? It's definitely not something he's prone to do, but I would hate to rain on his New Leaf parade.

The slammer door interrupts my thoughts and my mom barges into the visitation hall. She shoots her middle finger to the guard who accompanies her. Before the guard turns away, he sends hand signals to George that prompt him to station himself closer to my mother. It's like one of those just-in-case shuffles that teachers do with behavior kids sometimes. George's efforts don't go unnoticed by my mom.

"Screw you, George." She emphasizes his name, feeling stronger for knowing it.

I can tell that it's because of me, and only because of me, that George puts up with her crap. A few of the other prisoners giggle. I can appreciate how this dents George's credibility and it makes me feel bad.

My mother sits across from me.

For some weird reason, I choose to ... smile. It just felt right for a second —

"What?" my mother huffs.

"It's been a little while," I say. "I'm happy to see you."

"Look, I don't have anything to give you for your birthday, if that's what you're looking for."

"It isn't ... I'm not ... I just —"

"I'd like to ask you something," she starts.

I wait.

"Whose side are you on?" she finishes.

"I'm sorry?"

"I had to hear it from another chick in here that your father and Carly are a thing."

I swallow hard.

She leans in. "Do you know how that feels, Missy?"

"I didn't know that. I mean, I knew that —"

"See!" she butts in. "I knew you knew!"

"No, I mean, I knew she cut his hair, but —"

She slams the tabletop, "Are you that bloody stupid? Do you really think she was just cutting his hair?"

George comes closer. "Sit down."

"It was only one time," I say.

"They've been together for months, you idiot." My mother's words knock me down.

"Enough, Susanna," George warns.

My mother lowers her voice again. "I'm not worried though." Her eyes go two shades darker. "I got the message out there. Carly knows better now," she laughs.

We're both quiet for a while.

"Mom," I begin.

She just looks at me and shrugs. "Out with it."

"Let's have a staring contest."

My mother looks at me like I'm crazy, but she doesn't blink.

Game on.

"Don't be ridiculous, Missy," she scorns. "You're seventeen years old."

She's baiting me. She knows I'm sixteen.

But it's too easy. I keep staring at her.

"Missy, stop!" she looks away.

I don't. I lock my eyes on her so hard I fear they may burn a hole in the side of her head.

"I'm not going to talk to you until you stop," she warns me.

My eyes are on fire; I want to blink so bad. Tears glaze my eyeballs for momentary relief before they singe some more.

"Guard!" my mom hollers. "Take me back!"

I am a statue with a sudden surge of strength.

"Well, wasn't this a lovely visit with my stubborn offspring," she says as she stands up. She lunges inches from my face. "Boo!" she yells.

Close call, but my lids just open … wider.

George leads my mother away. She looks back at me and sees I've yet to succumb to the scalding pain in my eyes. I catch a glimpse of a slight smile on her lips.

I win.

The whole way home, I practice how to ask my father if Luke can come over. The experts would say to start with a joke:

Looks like we're both in relationships, huh Dad?

Scratch that.

So, Dad, now that I'm sixteen, I think it's time I start to explore men.

Too forward.

Dad, I really don't feel complete without spending time with this guy.
Too backward.

I'm almost at my house now. I scramble:

Dad, I respect you. So that's why I'd like to tell you a bit about the guy I'm hoping to spend some time with tonight, if it's okay with you.

Satisfied with that compromise and actual sincerity, I take a deep breath before I open the door to my house. My father isn't on the couch as I'd expect at this time.

"Hello?" I call out. "Dad?"

I walk through the whole house looking for him. He's nowhere to be seen.

I head to my room to make whatever adjustments for improvement I can to myself before Luke gets here.

But a knock at the front door limits me to Natural Me and I have no choice but to face Luke as is.

I run downstairs and peek out the window. It's Luke, all right. Unlike me, he made some adjustments on himself and damn, he looks super cute.

I open the door. "Hi," my voice squeaks higher than I've ever heard it.

Luke smiles. I'm warmed all over.

"What do you think about going for a bike ride?" he asks. "It's a great night."

"Oh ... um ... no, I just —"

"I know you have a bike. I saw it back there," Luke tries to convince me.

"I just don't feel like —"

"I thought we could ride to the canal," he says. "I packed you a birthday picnic." He turns to show me his stuffed backpack.

I melt a little.

"We can walk," I declare.

"Walk? What are you? Crazy? It's like three miles!"

"Luke —"

"Just take out your damn bike!"

"I will never ride a bike again!" I yell.

My Side of the Story

⋮

Luke and I sit across from each other on my back lawn, at sunset, sharing my birthday picnic. There's a buffet of strawberries, crackers, olives, peanut butter, and Pepsi. I'm pretty sure it's the best meal anyone's ever made for me.

"Are you ready to talk about it?" Luke asks me.

I take a bite of my strawberry.

"You don't have to, if you don't want to," he offers. "I mean, it's just not very often that you meet someone who vows to never ride a bike again." He smiles, but I can tell that it's not a making-fun smile.

"I tend to ... associate things." My throat closes up on my strawberry bits. I choke. Luke pats me on the back. It's embarrassing.

Once I regain composure I say, "I have a little brother. Had. I mean. I had a little brother."

"I heard," Luke says. "I heard you had a little brother and that he died. And I'm sorry."

I try to swallow the lump in my throat. It never works.

"Do you know how he died?" I ask.

"No, I don't. What was his name?" he asks.

"Jeremy." I can barely say it. Luke rubs my back now. I feel like I'm on another planet, looking in on us. "I'm glad you don't know how he died. It was my fault." A tear rolls down my cheek. Sneaky little bugger. I didn't even know it was there.

Luke sits up and leans in. "Listen to me and listen to me closely, Bell. There's nothing you can say or do that will make me think any less of you."

I look up at him. There are two things I want to do so badly right now. One is kiss him. The other is, for some asinine reason, I want to tell him everything.

"It was my thirteenth birthday and I was feeling all into myself," I admit.

"As thirteen-year-olds do," Luke says.

But they shouldn't.

"I used to walk Jeremy to school. It was one of my chores." I ache at the thought. I treated it like a chore and now I'd give anything to spend time with that little prince.

A few more tears spill freely. "Well, I was adamant that because I was thirteen, I should get to walk to school by myself. I fought with my parents so hard that morning. Usually I was a really obedient kid who never, ever mouthed off. I begged them to take Jeremy to school, even just this once, so that I could have some time to myself. Well, they refused."

I take a drink of my pop to try to force the lump aside. To no avail.

"When I walked out to the driveway, Jeremy had both of our bikes ready to go. He said, 'Let's ride to school today since I know how much you love that.' That in itself was so cute because he hated riding his bike. He said it made his 'two butts hurt.'" I laugh for a second, even though water pools in my eyes.

"He used to think he had two butts because of the two cheeks and no one wanted to correct him because it was so cute." I take a second to compose myself. "He even placed a bunch of crisp, yellow dandelion weeds on my bike seat and said, 'Those are for your birthday. I got them for you.' Being the selfish bitch I was, I picked them up and threw them over the fence. Then I flung my bike and smashed it against the fence. I told him that the last thing I wanted to do, on my birthday, was to have to take care of a little baby."

I put my head in my hands.

Luke sits closer to me and says, "If this is too hard, you don't have to say any more. It's super sad and it's your birthday and —"

"Then I got this bright idea. I told Jeremy that if he loved me and if he really wanted to give me something I'd actually like for my birthday, he'd let me walk to school by myself. He nodded his little head so hard, to please me." I take a few deep breaths. "I made him promise to stay right where he was, and then, and only when I was out of sight around the corner, he could go in to tell my mom and dad that they had to bring him."

My chest starts aching and constricting my breathing. I feel dizzy.

"Anyway, that's pretty much it," I say.

Luke looks like a series finale just left him with *to be continued.*
Awfully confused, he still says, "Okay."

"I want to tell you, but I'm afraid I'll cry," I say.

"You're already crying, Bell. And what's so wrong with that?
I'd be more freaked out if you weren't crying." He holds my hand.

My head starts swirling and my palms are sweaty in his.

"So off I walked. As I reveled in the freedom, Jeremy did exactly
as I instructed him. So much so that when my mom whipped out
of the house for some reason, he didn't say a peep. I ... I must not
have been fully out of his sight yet. I don't know." My breathing
intensifies. "I guess my mom got into her truck ... it was this stupid
beast of a truck ... and Jeremy ... he ... he was so little, and ..."

I cry.

Hard.

Luke hugs me and rocks me back and forth a little.

"The worst part is, no one knew he was ... hurt. The principal
told me Jeremy wasn't in class and that no one was answering
the phone at home. So I ran back to see what was going on and ...
there he was."

We hear a loud noise from inside my house.

I wipe the tears from my eyes and start to pack up the picnic.
"That could be my father. I'm sorry I didn't have a chance to ask
him if you could come over but —"

The back door flies open and smashes against the siding. My
father stands there and shields his eyes from the shed's motion
sensor light beam. "Missy?" he calls out.

I fear I hear a slur in his voice. My stomach flips.

"Yeah Dad, it's me. I'm back here with a friend I'd like you to meet." I act as cool as I can.

Luke starts to walk towards my dad with his hand extended for a handshake. "Hello, sir. I'm Luke."

Treat slaps Luke's hand away then looks at me with all of the picnic stuff in my hand. "What the hell is this?" he shouts.

"Dad, can I talk to you inside for a minute?" I urge.

"Let's just talk out here. The three of us." His *s*s are slithering snakes sauced up. He falls to the back steps and pretends it was on purpose. He composes himself. He looks at Luke. "What's your name again?"

"It's Luke," I say.

"The boy can talk for himself, Missy. No one likes a pushy woman that's gonna sit around and tell you what you can and can't do with your time or who you can or can't see when you wanna ..." His words trail off.

Luke looks at me and as he goes to say something, out of the corner of my eye, I see Treat pull a paper out of his pocket.

"I think I should go," Luke says. I start to walk him out of the yard.

"Hold it there a minute," Treat hollers at us. "Hey did you know my daughter is a great writer?" he asks.

What the hell is he up to?

Luke figures the question was meant for him. "No sir, I didn't actually. I mean, our teacher has shared some of her answers in our English class so —"

"You always talk this damn much?" Treat interrupts.

Luke's patience appears to thin.

Treat taps the paper in his hands, then scans the words until he finds what he's looking for. He reads aloud, using a super-feminine, valley-girl voice, "'The bus pass was a very sweet gift that I know cost you a lot of money,'" He looks up at me. "You're right. It did!" Then he looks back down at the letter and reads, "'It showed me that you respect my growing independence and you're giving me a chance to spread my wings.'" He looks over at Luke. "Now, isn't that sweet? Oh ... but wait for it ..." He glares at me again while he recites the closing line, "'That, or you just really want me to get a job.'"

Luke giggles despite himself.

My father holds up my bus pass.

"This ..." he shouts, "is now mine! You ungrateful piece of garbage."

"That was a joke, Dad. I just ... I thought the letter was getting heavy so I made a joke. That's what I do."

"That's what she does, sir." Luke supports me.

Treat crumples up the note and puts the bus pass in his pocket. He approaches Luke. "You think I don't know my own kid?"

Luke backs up a bit, trying to deflect the intimidation.

"I know my kid!" Treat yells. "My kid's the kind who rats me out to her mother!"

"I swear I didn't. She knew things I didn't even know." I panic.

"My kid's the kind who manipulates people to get what she wants." Treat walks within inches of Luke's face. "Don't you see that, Lion?"

Oh no.

"What did you say?" Luke isn't sure he heard that right.

"Dad!" I shout.

Treat laughs hysterically. "Like I said, kid, my daughter's a great writer. Even when she's pretending to be a dumb, imprisoned loser."

Luke stands his ground face to face with my intoxicated father, but his black eyes cloud over and tear up.

Before I can catch my breath from chest pains and lack of oxygen, Luke runs clear off of our lawn, hops on his bike and speeds away.

I charge at my father, fists first. I hit him over and over and over. "I hate you! I hate you so much!"

Treat tears me off of him and flings me against the shed.

"Leave her alone, Tim!" a distant neighbor shouts from his window.

"Mind your business!" Treat shouts back. He picks up the pile of picnic things and throws them at me. The Pepsi bottle smashes against the shed and a shard of glass rips through my shirt across my forearm.

Treat is mesmerized, frozen for a moment. I hope that he comes to. I want him to snap back to my father from this morning. I want him to be sorry for this cut on my arm, to be sorry for spilling my secret to Luke.

Because ... I would forgive him.

But he isn't.

He doesn't.

He just stumbles back towards the house, disappears into it, and slams the door shut.

And in that very moment, I decide that it's not my house anymore.

Loss

⋮

The whole way to the store, I have a sick feeling in my stomach. This isn't my worst birthday yet, of course — it's obvious which is my worst — but this one will go down in the books as pretty awful.

What kind of book is my life? What would the chapters be called? What would the cover look like? Who would read it?

No one.

For eight o'clock at night, it's awfully quiet out here. It's the kind of dark that hasn't been dark long but blankets the sky in its control and pulls no punches until stars poke through.

The only comfort I feel right now is the fond memories of all the times I fled to Ren's store for a feeling of safety and security. Like a worn stuffy you need at bedtime, Ren didn't have to speak to me or be perfect or do anything but except ... be there. I know he's only open for a couple more hours, but being in his presence will be the calm I need to figure out where I go next. Maybe I will be brave enough to ask him and Valkyrie if I can just huddle in a corner of the store for the night in a sleeping bag.

As I round the street corner, I feel like the night has become darker than ever. An eerie feeling washes over me. Is it the streetlights? Are they out? Is it because there aren't any cars on the road? Why does it feel like a metal slate looms overhead?

I realize what it is, and I don't like it one bit.

From here, I can see that the store's lights are out. I double-check my phone to see what time it is. Aside from a list of missed calls from some unknown number; no doubt telemarketers, I see it's indeed just after eight.

Something's not right.

I get a sinking feeling in my stomach, worried that Treat beat me here, that he came here in his drunken mess and caused trouble for Ren. I pick up speed and run to the store's doors.

The sign reads 'Closed' and all of the lights are out. I peek through the window and look as far back as I can to see if any of the back lights are on. I bang on the door. "Ren?" I shout. "Valkyrie?"

I back up a few steps to get a better vantage point of their upstairs apartment. Its lights are out, too.

Footsteps catch my attention. I turn my head, hoping to see Ren or Valkyrie, but it's just some kid and his mom.

Stubborn as a mule, I place my face against the store window again to see if I can see anything different than I did ten seconds earlier.

I feel a nudge against my leg.

I turn to see its source and then I recognize the Hot Wheels kid.

His mother speaks. "Joey and I saw you from our house," she says. "We wanted to come talk to you." She's much softer to me than the first time I met her, back when her son was begging for her to buy the Hot Wheels.

"I have something for you," little Joey says to me with a sly smile. He outstretches two handfuls of nickels and dimes. "I think that covers it." He giggles.

I let him pour the change into my hands. "Wow, look at you, paying all at once!" I am overly dramatic.

His mother holds open a baggie for me to put all of the change in, then says, "Well, he's been here a few times, but you two kept missing each other ... according to Mr. Lin."

I bend down to meet Joey eye-to-eye. "Well, you can be rest-assured Little Man. I'll get this money to Mr. Lin as soon as I can tomorrow." Joey's eyes light up like the weight of the world has been lifted from his shoulders.

His mother, on the other hand, looks like she's going to cry. Maybe this is a touching moment for her because her son is acting so mature and grown up?

"Can I talk to you over here for a second?" she asks me.

I go to shrug, but say, "Yes."

We walk out of earshot from Joey and he doesn't budge.

"I fear you haven't heard about Mr. Lin," the woman says.

Haven't heard what?

A dread tingles down from my head to my toes.

The woman does that whole sympathetic head tilt thing.

I look at the store front.

I look back at the woman.

I start to shake my head no.

She goes to put her hand on my shoulder.

I step back and shake my head more violently from side to side.

"It was a heart attack, honey. They said he didn't suffer at all," she offers.

"No!" I shout.

"Would you like to come to our place for a drink of water? You're very pale."

"When did this happen?!" I have trouble catching my breath.

"Monday afternoon," she says.

I sit down on the pavement and cry. She tries to help me back up.

"Please ... just leave me alone," I beg of her. She complies.

Before they head home, Joey comes over to me, pats me on the head a few times then sort of half hugs me with his little arms. It makes me cry harder.

Once they're far enough away, I bawl my eyes out. A puddle gathers from my falling tears into a river that trickles downward to Ren's Relics.

Homeless

⋮

I walk aimlessly for hours. I cry my tears dry. It's like there's nothing left inside of me. It's near eleven o'clock and I feel lost with no one looking for me.

Before I know it, I'm standing in front of my school. It's amazing how I've led myself to a place that I claim to hate but obviously represents some kind of security to my subconscious.

I look up at the massive building. It looks different at night — peaceful and strong. I eye the windows and wonder how thick they are. I just need a place to crash, somewhere that I can't be hurt by strangers or eaten by coyotes.

I can see a few lights on inside and I presume they're security lights that stay on all night. The reason I know this is because sitting on the office bench one day, I overheard the secretary saying it was time to replace the bulbs, like they do every year around that time.

I tiptoe up to a side window and take some time to survey my environment. The nearby houses aren't close enough to see me and the streetlights illuminate the opposite side of the school. My detective work yields the go-ahead for my little break-and-enter plan as fatigue renders my Better Sense comatose.

I feel around on the ground for some time before I find a rock that I deem big enough to do some real damage. It's only about the size of my heart, but it should do the trick. To muffle the sound, I take off my bra and wrap it around the rock before I smash it against the window. It does nothing, not even a chip.

I try again.

It hurts my hand.

I stop to compose myself. I think for a moment about this birthday, my last birthday, and, of course, my dreaded birthday before that one. I think about my father and his disregard of my trust. I think about my mother and the ignorance of her actions and lack of affection. I think about Ren's weak, dumbass heart and how it, most of all, has betrayed me. I hold my hand back behind my head. I concentrate all of my anger, sadness, and energy to power one final hurl and —

My hand is stopped. Mid-air.

I scream and spin around to see —

Miss Maalouf. "Missy!" she says. "What are you trying to do?"

I start shaking at the interrupted release. I convulse with the rush of adrenaline. Miss Maalouf doesn't wait for an answer, she just takes the rock out of my hand, drops it to the ground and hugs me tighter than anyone has in ages.

❖

The whole drive to her house, Miss Maalouf talks about the weather, her new night shift, the adjustments she's made for the kids, and her challenges and woes. She fills the air with words because I haven't said one since the moment she saw me.

As we pull up to her house, I study its curb appeal. The place is tiny but cute. It's not at all fancy, but it's charming.

Miss Maalouf turns off the car. "Listen Missy, I don't know what's up with you or where your head's at, but I'm just glad you stopped shaking. You're welcome to stay in the car, or come in, or I can drive you home."

I shake my head no.

"Why don't you come in so I can give you a warm glass of milk," she says.

I watch her go to her house and eventually let someone who must be her nanny out the front. The nanny looks like she's about a million years old. A cab pulls up on the street to pick her up.

I sit in Miss Maalouf's car for a while, considering my options. I see Miss Maalouf, now in her PJ's, as she peeks out through her front window curtains at me.

I surrender. I open the car door and head into her house.

The moment I'm in, she wraps a blanket around my shoulders. On the coffee table, as promised, there's a tall glass of milk and a plate with cheese and crackers on it.

I look at Miss Maalouf. I open my mouth to say thank you, but nothing comes out.

"I'm going to go to bed," she states. "Morning comes early around here. If you need the washroom, there's a two-piece around the corner. If you want to take a bath or a shower, head to the top of the stairs and turn right. Help yourself to anything in the cupboards or fridge," she offers.

I shake my head no.

"Missy, please stop. You're obviously going through enough. Trying to please me with the right words or please yourself with some kind of stubborn pride isn't important right now. If you're ready to go home in a bit, wake me and I will summon you a cab. My treat. If the couch feels comfortable, sleep on it. If not, there's a spare bed up in the office to the left upstairs. My son may wake up in the middle of the night, though. He's been doing that since my new shift started. He hates the nanny," she shrugs.

With the twist of a couple door locks and flicks of some light switches, it's safe and dark except for a nightlight in the kitchen and one lamp by the couch.

Miss Maalouf places a phone charger on the table by my milk and walks upstairs.

I take a sip of the milk, but think about Ren for a minute and then I can't swallow. I spit the milk back into the glass. The cheese and crackers look delicious, but the thought of eating them makes my stomach turn. The couch and pillow look most inviting. I just want to lie down and try to take my mind off of everything.

I lie still, completely awake and wide-eyed. I try to count. I try to put all of my body parts to sleep like Dr. Tandalay once tried to teach me to do. I try to take long inhales and exhales, but I simply cannot turn my mind off.

I hear footsteps on the stairs and wonder why Miss Maalouf is still up. I turn to see her, but it's her daughter, Aahana.

I'm terrified she's going to scream at the sight of a stranger on her couch, but she just tilts her head to get a better look at me. She narrows in on my face. I sit up slowly so that she can get a better look. Once I sense vague familiarity, I wave gently.

She waves back. She takes a few steps towards me and sits on the floor. "Hi," she whispers.

"Hi," my voice cracks. I haven't said anything in hours.

"What's your name again?" she asks.

"Missy," I say.

"Do you remember my name?" she wonders.

"Yes, I do, Aahana."

She smiles. I guess it's true; people do like the sound of their own name.

"Aren't you supposed to be in bed?" I whisper.

"Why are you sleeping over?" she asks. I admire her deflection skills.

"I needed somewhere to stay," I answer.

"You don't have a mom?" she asks me. I'm struck by her question. She associates me not having a place to stay with not having a mom. Not only that, but she doesn't seem too concerned about a dad, which leads me to believe she doesn't have one in the picture. "I have a mom. I just don't really have a house right now. It's kind of hard to explain," I probably said more than I needed to.

"Can I sit with you?" Aahana asks.

"Sure." I surprise myself with the ease and sincerity of my answer.

Aahana hops onto the couch and helps herself to half of the blankets. Her level of comfort and lack of social inhibitions remind me of how adorably ignorant and bold Jeremy was at her age.

"Okay, goodnight," Aahana says as she lays down against her end of the couch.

I laugh. I don't know what to do. Leave her there? Get Miss Maalouf? Tell Aahana she can't sleep down here? She looks so peaceful and content that I just watch her for a few moments. An unbelievable wave of exhaustion washes over me and I just ... put ... my head ... onto the great pillow ... and ...

Wait, What

.
.
.

I woke up this morning and wanted to avoid school like the plague, but here I am. I decided to just deal with it. What's the worst that could happen? Luke might pick me up and throw me out a window, but our school is only two stories high. I figured I'd survive. The walk to English is a long one.

The morning was interesting at Miss Maalouf's. Since she's on a night shift, she gets to spend the day with her two kids. Krish takes up a lot of her attention. He's a real sweetheart with his affection for his momma.

When Miss Maalouf woke me up, I had no idea where I was. I was in a deep sleep, so I jumped at her touch. She got a real kick out of the sight of Aahana at my feet. I thought she'd be mad, but now I'm starting to think this woman never gets mad, except at her nanny and Mr. Mianni.

Krish and Aahana crawled onto my lap for most of the morning, then when it was time for me to leave for school, I couldn't thank Miss Maalouf enough. Between the cozy set-up and hospitality, the breakfast, the change of clothes and the company, I felt spoiled. When Miss Maalouf said what she said next, my heart nearly burst.

"You're welcome to stay anytime, Missy."

Part of me wanted to wave her off and act aloof like I didn't want or need her help. However, an overpowering part of me just smiled and told her that I might take her up on that.

I finished folding up the blankets and sheet and piled them on the coffee table. Both of the kids hugged me and, in that moment, an idea struck me that made all the sense in the world. I made sure I was far enough away from the kids so that they couldn't hear me. "Miss Maalouf," I started, "what if, to pay you back for letting me crash here for a while ... well ... what if I watch your kids while you work?"

"Yes!" Aahana screamed from the other room.

Both Miss Maalouf and I laughed. "I guess you're hired!" Miss Maalouf stated. "That would be ... incredible."

Aahana ran into the living room and hugged my leg. Krish had absolutely no idea what all the commotion was about but, he copied his big sister's actions and hugged my other leg. For but a moment, my cup was overfilled.

But now a feeling of dread consumes me as I approach my English class. This is the moment of truth. I imagine Luke blowing a basketball-sized spitball at my head upon my entry.

But he's not here.

What I thought would be great relief is actually a weird pain in my chest. I find my seat and settle in helplessly, for more of *The Great Gatsby*.

As I walk down the hallways after class, my heart starts racing when I approach the office windows, where Luke usually waits on the bench to meet with Ms. FACS. I hold my breath and turn my head slightly to see if I spot him and ...

He's not there, either. Where the hell is he?

I push open the school's front doors and lead a bunch of pent-up teenagers to freedom. Everyone fans out in separate directions, off to do their own things.

I reach the sidewalk and turn to walk to Miss Maalouf's when a hand grabs my shoulder. I turn around and see —

Valkyrie.

Shock consumes me. Then pain. The sight of her reminds me so much of Ren that tears build.

Then I stop and think. This moment isn't really about me. I step forward and hug Valkyrie — a gesture I never imagined myself doing. "I'm so sorry," I whisper in her ear.

Valkyrie is one of the strongest women I've ever known and she doesn't disappoint in this moment. She takes in the hug and accepts it. Then she pushes me away to compose herself before she talks.

"I tried to call you," she says.

Flashes of unknown caller notifications dizzy me. "I'm so sorry," I say. "Had I known you were calling, I —"

"I get it. It's fine. I just don't want you to think that I didn't want you involved, that I didn't want you to know what happened. It all happened ... so fast," she chokes up.

I nod my head.

"Is there a funeral?" I asked her.

"Yes. But not here. In China," Valkyrie says. "It's tradition to do it there, with all of our relatives. We don't really know anyone here, my father especially. He only really knew ... you."

That makes my heart ache. Valkyrie sees the tears in my eyes and she gets noticeably uncomfortable. She elects to take an envelope out of her purse. She hands it to me.

I take it and study my barely legible and misspelled name on the outside: "Misy".

"It's from my dad," Valkyrie says. "I found it in his office."

I hold it against my chest. "Thank you," I say.

"You're not going to know what it says," Valkyrie laughs. "He spoke a mean English, but written, not so much."

I carefully pry the envelope open. The beauty of the Chinese penmanship on the paper inside awes me. I run my finger along the words.

Then it hits me. "Wait a minute. I was told that your dad had a heart attack. I don't understand how —"

"I don't understand it either," Valkyrie looks down. After a long pause, she says, "I was always jealous of your relationship with my father. I've never seen two people be so close even though they were worlds away. But that doesn't excuse how rude I was to you sometimes and I'm sorry."

I'm at a loss for words.

"Anyway, just let me read it to you," Valkyrie grabs the paper from my hands. My heart shouts *be careful!*

Valkyrie looks down at the page and even she studies the grace and love in the penmanship. I fear for a second that she's going to rip it up, but she just sighs and starts to read it to me. "*I'm writing this because, after the events of the other night, I'm sure your father will never allow you to visit the store again. As a father myself, I understand that and forgive him. But I cannot go without letting you know these important things, so I decided to write you this letter. Sometimes, in life, something or someone becomes part of you that you never imagined would be as wonderful as it is. That for me, is —*" Valkyrie stops, chokes up, then composes herself, "*— my baby Val. She is the blood of my blood and a precious gem to me. But then one day, out of nowhere, Buddha blessed me with a lone star. A young girl drifted into my soul. I don't know what, in reality, led you to me that day because you never once talked about it. You sure talked a lot about other things though: your parents, your lack of friends, your pet peeves, and then that Skywalker boy —*"

I blush.

Valkyrie notices then looks back at the paper, "*Whatever it was that happened to you was tragic and life-changing, but it never changed You. You never stopped being the loyal girl who showed up six times a week. You never stopped being the creative girl who impressed passersby with window displays. You never stopped being the kind girl who made customers smile. You never stopped being the selfless girl who asked for absolutely nothing in return, ever. I thought I was an expert on invaluable things, until I had Valkyrie. Then again when I had you. Whether or not you ever visit the store again, you will always hold residence in my heart where you'll remain safe and loved forever.*"

Valkyrie folds up the letter and looks up at me as tears stream down my face. She tucks the letter back into its envelope and hands it to me. I'm sure she's going to walk away any minute, but she doesn't. She just stands there.

She wipes tears from her eyes. "Okay," she starts. "Do you think we can just stop crying for a second?"

I try, but it's hard. She gives me a minute. I manage to dam the flood.

"I have something to tell you and ... it's really something," Valkyrie says.

Dear gawd. I cannot handle more bad news at this point. I fear it will be the end of me.

Valkyrie flips her backpack around and opens it up. She pulls out a white portfolio folder, like the kind I use to submit really important English essays. "We're ... ummm ... I'm ... selling the store because it's just not my dream, as much as my father may have hoped it to be. So I've been talking with the bank and lawyers and all kinds of crap."

I don't know why she's telling me this. Maybe she just needs someone to vent to?

"It's earlier than he wanted, but the lawyers have this, for when it's time to settle the bill," Valkyrie says. She opens the portfolio. "At first, I was dead set against this idea, so dead set against it, my father and I didn't talk for months —"

I flash back to a time I remember Valkyrie and Ren fighting. It didn't happen very often, but I remember one time specifically when I was pretty new to them. I was working away on pricing and stocking and the two of them passed by each other without words or gestures for what felt like forever. Ren looked heartbroken and Valkyrie looked like a little devil of glaring eyes and dirty looks directed at her father and me.

"Missy?" Valkyrie waves a hand in front of my face. "Did you hear me?"

"Oh ... no. I'm sorry. I was thinking about something."

"All right then ... let me try this again." She clears her throat. "My father's been putting away an hourly wage for you, for every hour you worked for him." She hands me a piece of paper from the portfolio. I don't look at it. I don't quite comprehend what she's saying. "Missy, this part is very important," she waits until I make eye contact. "The lawyers won't release the money to you until you're eighteen. An adult."

It's like I'm in some kind of a daze, like she's talking to me but I'm not in my body. I'm floating overhead like a bird and swooping in and out of her words. Maybe I accidentally took a double dose of my medication this morning?

"Missy? Are you okay?" Valkyrie wonders.

I finally do it. I look down at the paper. My eyes scan a bunch of words and signatures and names and dates and fine print but then ... I see a number.

Valkyrie gauges my reaction. "Three years ... six days a week ... four or five hours a night, give or take ... minimum wage. I think it's a fair valuation."

I've never seen that many digits in a line behind a dollar sign except for stupid problem-solving questions in math class. I stare at the number and shake my head. I go to hand the paper back to Valkyrie.

"This isn't charity kid. Don't you dare try to hand that back to me."

I don't know what to do. I'm frozen, but overheating.

"If it weren't for you, I'd have had to be doing all that stuff. You gave me the space to be able to study and concentrate on school and sports and a social life. And as much as I hate to admit it, you helped fill a void in my father that my mother left and that I was too selfish to acknowledge. Between both of us, I think he was content," Valkyrie packs up her things. "In two years, just hire yourself a lawyer and that's yours. Can you manage, until then?"

Aahana and Krish flash in my mind. "Yes," I say.

I somehow manage to say, "I'll be sure to subtract roughly twelve hundred dollars from it."

Valkyrie pauses for a moment.

"The window." She laughs almost inaudibly. She turns to walk away then stops to look back at me. "Don't be a stranger. I'm keeping the apartment above the store. I'm sure my father would get a real kick out of it if we sat and watched his show together sometime, or something." With a quick, two-finger salute, Valkyrie leaves.

Break On Through

⋮

I walk into Dr. Tandalay's office and head over to the receptionist's counter. I reach for the sign-in clipboard.

"What are you doing?" he asks.

"Signing in," I say.

"You don't have to do that anymore," he says.

"Oh," I say. "What about the fire code?" I smirk.

"The fire department just doesn't care about your well-being
anymore," he shrugs.

I look down at the list of names. "But they care about all of these
other people?" I retort.

I smile and sign my name and in-time. Just as the time on my
phone clicks to the hour, efficient Dr. Tandalay releases a patient
and wishes the man a good week. She turns to me and smiles.

◆

With only fifteen minutes left in the appointment, I wish we had a bit more time. I feel like I've talked forever today but there's still so much more to tell her. I got through all my week's downfalls and delights and dizzied myself with details. I take a very deep breath.

"Thank you for sharing all of that with me," Dr. Tandalay says. "I obviously have some paperwork to do and need to update FACS on your new living arrangement and how great it's going."

"Okay, thank you," I say.

"Have you talked to your father lately?" she asks.

"I plan to soon," I say.

"Missy, can I ask you something?" she leans in.

Like I can stop you.

"How in line with your thoughts are your words and actions?" she asks.

I look at her. Then I peek at the clock.

"Don't worry about what time it is," she says.

"I don't know what you mean."

"You know what I mean. How in line with your thinking is what you say and do?"

Hardly ever.

I stare at her. She stares back. I wait for her to blink first.

"Hardly ever," I breathe.

Dr. Tandalay leans back. She doesn't say anything for a while.

"Relax your breathing, Missy. You're safe here. You're doing great." Dr. Tandalay smiles.

"Doing great?" I laugh.

"Yes," she sounds so convinced. "You know, sometimes, when trauma is suffered at an early age, our brain fragments to help us cope. It kind of builds an army of selves to help you deal."

"I didn't suffer trauma." I'm hardly listening to her. "I caused it."

The room starts to fade to black on me.

"Take a few deep breaths, Missy." It sounds like she's far away but I hear her. I take a few deep breaths and the room is light again.

"You think it's your fault? You believe you're the reason Jeremy died?" She voices the words from the pit of my dark soul.

I start to shake and my chest hurts.

"Keep taking deep breaths, Missy."

I forget to, and then I remember.

Dr. Tandalay wraps me in a blanket and sprays some kind of essential oil by my nose.

I look up at the clock.

"Stop worrying about the time," she says. "Tell me what you're thinking."

"I'm not worried about the time. I just want out of here!" I shout.

"Part of you is scared and trying to protect you. You can calm that part of you. I'm here to protect you too."

A calm washes over me and I shake a little less.

"You were just a child when Jeremy died," she tries.

"I was thirteen," I shout.

"A child." She's adamant. "Despite what you believed at the time, you were a child, Missy. You were a child behaving as children do. Egocentric. Stubborn. Naive."

I don't know why I feel so mad at her right now.

"I know I'm making a part of you very angry right now."

What the —

"You know who wasn't a child when Jeremy died, Missy? Your

parents. They were adults." She leans in and looks directly into my eyes. "Missy —"

Why does she keep saying my damn name?

"What do you remember about your adult parents from that morning?"

I clench my teeth. "How many times do I have to tell you that I don't want to talk about that day?"

"I think you're more ready to now than you've ever been. C'mon Missy. What do you remember about your parents that morning?"

I start to think about my mom and dad in their bedroom ...

"Out loud, Missy," Dr. Tandalay orders.

"I don't really remember. All I can think of is them being in their room, in bed," I say sincerely.

Dr. Tandalay's tone switches. I think of it as her reading-a-book voice. "Sometimes, trauma survivors can remember. Sometimes they can't. And then they can again. Other times, we try to forget things that hurt us."

"I just forget because it was three years ago," I retort.

"What were you wearing that day?" she asks.

Damn it. I can remember the exact outfit I had on.

I shrug, then I know better.

"I can remember my outfit," I rectify.

Dr. Tandalay opens up a very thick file folder dedicated to lil' ol' me. As she leafs through a few pages at the front of it, she continues her query. "Did you ask your parents to bring Jeremy to school for you that morning?"

"Yes. I begged them like crazy." I look up at the clock. Thank the lord there's only a minute left.

"I don't have a patient after you, Missy." Dr. Tandalay puts an end to that.

"I just wanted to walk to school by myself, to celebrate becoming a teenager. That's all I remember."

"How did your parents celebrate you … your birthday, that morning?"

All I can see is Jeremy, our bikes and a fistful of yellow dandelions.

"I don't remember," I say.

She reads over some paper in her hand. "You had to talk to the police that day. I have the whole transcript here. You're not ready to read it yet, but one day you will be. For now, I'd like to tell you that, according to this, they did nothing that morning."

I shrug, because truly, I'm not surprised and I don't care.

"Missy, what you did was normal. You made decisions that morning that ninety-nine percent of kids in your situation would have made. You protected and loved and cared for that little boy his entire life, yet all you think of is the one day you begged to have a little time to yourself so that you could celebrate being a teenager."

I look down.

"Do you know why your parents said no, Missy?"

"Because I just should have done what I was told and not talk back?" I say.

"Because they were highly intoxicated and under illegal influences," she asserts.

"No," I say. "They didn't start all that stuff until after I killed Jeremy."

Dr. Tandalay holds up a different piece of paper. "This is a toxicology report. Your dad couldn't even get out of bed that morning. Your mom …"

My head spins.

"Your mom, Missy, was five times over the legal drinking limit when she pulled out of the driveway that morning."

My heart punches the walls of my chest. My brain bangs my temples.

"Your mother in is in jail because of that. Unfortunately, your fifteenth birthday was her day of reckoning. They reached a sentence for manslaughter."

"My MacBook. It was because of my MacBook," I mutter.

"Your MacBook? Dear gawd Missy. That was simply a coincidence."

"And you waited to tell me that?" I yell.

"First of all, I didn't know you believed that. Second, I wasn't permitted to tell you details about your mom until you were sixteen. But, most importantly, you weren't ready to hear it. You've never even been able to talk to me about Jeremy without an anxiety attack, until today."

Which I'm on the verge of having now.

"Missy, it's fascinating. Humans tend to remember the things they need to, how they need to, to survive. I'm here to help you get through this. You're going to get through this. You have one of the brightest futures ahead of you of any of my patients."

I look up at her.

"Please don't tell any of them that I just said that." She laughs.

I half-smile. For some reason, I believe her.

A New Chapter

⋮

I walk with my new meds prescription in my hand. Dr. Tandalay decreased the milligrams. I asked her three times if she was sure that that was the right thing to do. I swear sometimes I think she's the crazy one.

I walk with a foreign skip in my step, towards the Maaloufs'.

Miss Maalouf told me that I don't need to bring much of anything to her house and that I can access anything at my disposal. Even her wardrobe, which is beautiful and she's totally willing to share with me. We're the same size, seeing as I'm so tall for my age and all. When I promised her that I would pay her back one day, she insisted that my rent, my meals, and my clothes would be covered in exchange for the babysitting. Little does she know that since she's technically my guardian now, she's going to get a monthly allowance from the government. I can't wait to tell her about it. It's a win-win. I try not to think about it too much because I'm scared I will jinx it.

I decide to redirect myself. I'd like to go to my father's house for just a few small things first. I brace myself for a conversation with him that I'm scared to have. He already knows I moved out, but there's been no depth to our exchanges in ages. As I walk, I draft a text of what I will say to him, in case he's not home.

I walk into the house after noticing the door isn't locked and there he is, on the couch, snoring away. A skunky, musky smell permeates the house.

I walk upstairs to my room and look around for what I want to take with me that will fit in my backpack. I start with some bras, underwear and socks, my favorite pens, some way overdue books from the library that I've adopted illegally and finally, Jeremy's Hot Wheels.

I head downstairs and consider waking up my father, but I think better of it. I have no idea who I will get: Trick or Treat.

I go to hit send on the text, but re-read the words I poured into it about him and my mother. I think better of sending it. He's not ready yet.

I save the text to the bottomless pit of drafts and send him another message instead: *Call me, if you want.* His phone dings its receipt and he doesn't even budge.

I feel it's safe to kiss him on the forehead so I do. I take in the familiar smell of his face and whiskers and blue-collar self. For a moment, I remember sitting on his lap and listening to CDs that brought him joy.

I walk out the front door and lock it behind me to keep him safe.

I turn around and see Luke, on his bike, on my front lawn.

The air is thick. My knees go weak.

I look everywhere but in his eyes.

"Where've you been?" he asks.

I don't answer straight away.

"You have this really annoying habit of not being where I want you to be," he says.

Where do you —

"Where do you want me to be?" I ask.

Now he's the one who doesn't answer straight away.

"I'm moving out," I say.

"Good," he says.

"Listen Luke —"

"No, you listen, Bell. I already told you. There's nothing you can say, or do, that would make me feel any less of you."

I blush madly and look at the ground.

"You did what you did. Am I thrilled about being played like that? No. Do I wish you were honest with me? Of course. But is it the most incredible thing anyone's ever done for me and my mom? Hands down."

And just like that, I'm in love.

But I clearly have no idea what to do about it.

I start by walking down the steps.

Luke gets off of his bike and I notice he's in his KFC uniform. Only he could make it look so attractive.

"Starting your shift or just ended it?" I ask.

Luke puts his hands in my hair and looks deep into my eyes. The black narrows in and wins me over. I can't help myself; I swear my smile takes up half of my face. We meet halfway and our lips touch. It's gentle and warm and familiar and safe and mutual and amazing.

"So where's home?" he asks.

In that kiss.

Some things are better left in your head probably.

"Miss Maalouf's," I laugh.

He's taken aback for a minute and then he shakes his head and laughs. "Only you, Bell. Only you."

"Tell me where and hop on. I'll double you there," he taps his bike seat.

I consider it, for a moment. Miss Maalouf's is a fair hike.

But I opt not to. I look back towards the backyard and eye the shed.

I walk to the back. Luke follows me.

I open the shed and look to where my bike used to be and it's gone!

"That son of a —"

Luke covers my mouth and laughs. He holds my hand and takes me out of the shed and points to the back of my house and there —

Is my bike. Upright. Sparkling clean.

"I knew you'd be ready one day, but it was not ready for you," Luke smiles. "Tires are good now. Brakes tested. Chain oiled."

I walk up to my bike. I run my finger along the edges of it and notice how it seems smaller but still so awesome. I truly did love riding this thing. Jeremy and I would rush out of the driveway and head to the park to play tag and Frisbee and hide-and-go-seek ... daily until dusk.

I wipe a tear from my eye.

"When you're ready," Luke whispers.

I think I'm ready.

I walk my bike to the front of the house and feel a bit sick to my stomach. Luke reads my face and hands me a drink from his water bottle. It actually helps.

I take a few very deep breaths before I heave my leg over the bike and cradle it between my thighs.

Luke prepares his bike beside me. He hops on his. "There's nothing to it," he says. "It's like ... riding a bike."

I use my power to lift onto the seat and I wobble uncontrollably for a few seconds before I steady myself. I push the pedals to gain momentum, then I push them harder to gain speed.

The wind rushes through my hair as Luke and I weave in and out of line with each other and as we pass by a massive field of bright, yellow dandelions, I just know it's going to be okay.

Acknowledgements

It is an honor for me to acknowledge that the land on which I live, work and write is the traditional territory of the Haudenosaunee and Anishinaabe peoples. The territory is covered by the Upper Canada Treaties and is within the land protected by the Dish with One Spoon Wampum agreement. The gathering place is home to many First Nations, Métis, and Inuit peoples and this acknowledgement reminds us that our ideal standard of living is directly related to Indigenous people.

I apologize in advance for my rather lengthy acknowledgements. Seeing as this is my debut novel (and hopefully not my last), I'd like to squeeze in as many people as I can who were part of this work's development and publication.

My love of writing started way back in grade five when Mrs. Laura O'Reilly told me that I "should be a writer when I grow up" after

I wrote a tragic tale of a child who succumbed to cancer. My short stories & poetry eventually turned into screenplays & manuscripts but one thing remained unchanged; writing is my catharsis and I'm blessed by this chance to get it into your hands.

I would love to acknowledge the family and friends who supported me through my *White Lies* journey. Thank you to Isaac (Payton), Ava and Marc for giving me the space to create, especially when I know my Mom-hat was a little off. Thank you to my late mother, Lauretta, for being my main cheerleader even back when she called my screenplays "novels" and hoped I'd win a Grammy for them. Thank you to Susan and Boyd for always going above and beyond. Thank you to my siblings: Bobbie, Dan and Nick, their partners and my nieces and nephews for taking the time to always ask about what was brewing and for talking me up. I appreciate my close friends for keeping me focused but also for charming me out of the house when I needed it (most especially Chrissy, Susan, Dana, Chrys, Teresa, Amy, Stephanie, Mallory, and the Traceys). Special thanks to Anna, Carlee, Nicole, Nadine, Kathy, Dr. Janina Fisher, Nicole LePera, Dr. Tan-Wilson and Dr. Csanadi for stimulating and/or nurturing my own personal health and healing.

Professionally, it is important to me to acknowledge Box for mentoring me throughout the last decade of my writing endeavours. Thank you to Eric Walters and Kelly Anne Blount for offering me guidance with *White Lies*, even though you had ten million other things to do. I cannot forget my incredible Twitter writing community for the many 140-character snippets of wisdom and inspiration. Finally, thank you to my supportive colleagues and over 700 students from my teaching career. I hope that my students believe me now, more than ever, that with extra hard work & persistence, it is possible.

The publication of *White Lies* is a direct result of a reassuring nudge from a wonderful teaching ally, Lynne Jensen. From then on, the devotion and care of DCB/Cormorant books (with the dedication & talent of publisher Barry Jowett, copy editor Sarah Jensen and Managing Director Sarah Cooper), brought it to life. I will forever be grateful to all of you for taking a chance on me, and on Missy's story.

Finally, and quite importantly, thank you to all of you for joining Missy for a few months of her life. Through her story, I hope sincerely that you are encouraged to nourish your own mental health with the self-care, compassion and explicit love you deserve.

Sara de Waard is an author and screen-writer of Métis descent and is currently in the process of exploring her family's heritage. She is an elementary school teacher and freelance social media manager with a love for film and a soft spot for rap and hip-hop music thanks to her two teenagers. Her writing is often inspired by her compassion for the trials and tribulations of today's youth. After completing her BA in Radio and Television from Ryerson University and a stint in London, Ontario, de Waard returned to her hometown of Port Colborne, Ontario where she currently lives with her kids.

We acknowledge the sacred land on which Cormorant Books operates. It has been a site of human activity for 15,000 years. This land is the territory of the Huron-Wendat and Petun First Nations, the Seneca, and most recently, the Mississaugas of the Credit River. The territory was the subject of the Dish With One Spoon Wampum Belt Covenant, an agreement between the Iroquois Confederacy and Confederacy of the Ojibway and allied nations to peaceably share and steward the resources around the Great Lakes. Today, the meeting place of Toronto is still home to many Indigenous people from across Turtle Island. We are grateful to have the opportunity to work in the community, on this territory.

We are also mindful of broken covenants and the need to strive to make right with all our relations.